THE CHRISTMAS LIGHT

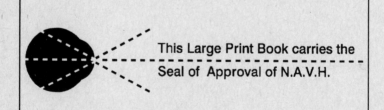

THE CHRISTMAS LIGHT

DONNA VANLIERE

THORNDIKE PRESS
A part of Gale, Cengage Learning

GALE
CENGAGE Learning·

Farmington Hills, Mich • San Francisco • New York • Waterville, Maine
Meriden, Conn • Mason, Ohio • Chicago

GALE
CENGAGE Learning®

Copyright © 2014 by Donna VanLiere.
Thorndike Press, a part of Gale, Cengage Learning.

ALL RIGHTS RESERVED
This is a work of fiction. All of the characters, organizations, and events portrayed in this novel are either products of the author's imagination or are used fictitiously.
Thorndike Press® Large Print Basic.
The text of this Large Print edition is unabridged.
Other aspects of the book may vary from the original edition.
Set in 16 pt. Plantin.

LIBRARY OF CONGRESS CATALOGING-IN-PUBLICATION DATA

VanLiere, Donna, 1966-
    The Christmas light / Donna VanLiere. — Large print edition.
      pages cm — (Thorndike press large print basic)
    ISBN 978-1-4104-7343-1 (hardback) — ISBN 1-4104-7343-0 (hardcover)
    1. Single parents—Fiction. 2. Teenage girls—Fiction. 3. Married people—Fiction. 4. Large type books. 5. Christmas stories. I. Title.
PS3622.A66C4785 2014b
813'.6—dc23   2014034922

Published in 2014 by arrangement with St. Martin's Press, LLC

Printed in the United States of America
1 2 3 4 5 6 7 18 17 16 15 14

For Barbara McGee,
who keeps finding the light in dark places

ACKNOWLEDGMENTS

Many thanks to:

Troy, Gracie, Kate, David, Lucy, CoCo, Katrina, and Cindy for keeping life exciting and full.

Jen Enderlin, the St. Martin's sales staff, and Michael Storrings for continued belief, outstanding work, and an amazing cover!

Julie Cranston, Dorothy Ley, Maren Milligan, Janice Churchill, Crystal Lepping, and Paige Mathias for your heart.

And a special thanks to the many readers I have met or heard from over the years. You are gracious and encouraging and it is a privilege to write for you. I hope you enjoy *The Christmas Light* as much as I enjoyed writing it.

In order for the light to shine so brightly, the darkness must be present.
— FRANCIS BACON

One

Maybe you have to know darkness before you can appreciate the light.
— MADELEINE L'ENGLE

Jennifer De Luca sits at the kitchen table and reaches for the phone, dialing the number in front of her. Although six-year-old Avery is playing in her room, the house is quiet. It is always still but sometimes, thankfully, the silence is louder than the noise in Jen's head. She listens to the phone ring in her ear. Over three years later, she still has more questions than answers but Dr. Becke says that all profound answers start with deep questions. "So much of life is made up of questions that we think matter a great deal today but are forgotten tomorrow," Dr. Becke said a few weeks ago. "But it's the life and death questions, the meaning, purpose, and value questions that matter." She looked at Jen in her office that day and smiled in a sad way that told Jen that some questions might never be answered.

The phone clicks on the other end and Jennifer follows the prompts for the main receptionist. "Dr. Schwartz's office, please," she says. She is transferred and is greeted by a recorded message. She'll have to leave a voice mail. "Hi, this is Jennifer De Luca, calling about my husband, Michael." When she hears Avery padding down the hall toward the kitchen, she cuts the message short. Avery stands in the kitchen doorway and pushes a mass of curls out of her face. Jennifer smiles, thinking how she and Michael laughed on seeing Avery's red, curly hair the day she was born.

"Where did that come from?" Michael asked, laughing. They reasoned it had to be one of their great-grandparents, whom neither had met. "You don't see many redheads," he said, reaching for his newborn. "She's a standout already."

"Who were you talking to?" Avery asks.

"No one. I was leaving a message for a woman."

Avery narrows her eyes and comes closer to her mom. "What woman?"

Jen sighs. "At the hospital."

"About Dad?"

"Yes." She gets up and opens a cupboard, changing the subject. "Would you like a snack before we leave?"

Avery shakes her head. "I'm not hungry." She's holding the angel doll she received from a stranger three and a half years ago. It's dressed in a shimmering pink dress with iridescent wings and long, flowing brown hair. Avery saw glimpses of the stranger but can't remember his face. She holds the doll tighter to her chest. She's been holding tightly to it since the stranger gave it to her, sleeping with it and bringing it in the car for the ride to and from school.

She walks to her mom and holds out her hand, opening it. Inside is Jennifer's wedding ring. "You forgot to put this on."

Jen's gray-blue eyes are rimmed in sadness. "I didn't forget, babe."

The small hand is held open in front of Jennifer. "Yes you did. You forgot it in your jewelry box." Her eyes are a mixture of confusion and pain and Jennifer feels her heart slip a little. She reaches for the ring and puts it on. "If you keep it on, you won't forget it."

Jen nods and kisses her daughter's forehead. "All right, let's go." Avery reaches for her coat and her favorite rainbow-colored scarf before getting into the car. The sky is gray and the tree branches reach into the sky like stripped nerves. A hunger for color seizes Jen. In her opinion winter hung on too long, often growing tiresome and sullen with its chilling winds and early nights. She looks in the rearview mirror and watches Avery. She's looking at the Christmas decorations lining the street and in the storefront windows but isn't seeing them. "It's as if I'm driving down a dark road," Jennifer thinks. She remembers that as a child, this time between the holidays was a sweet and anticipated gift, where time almost seemed suspended, sparkling and magical. She wonders what Avery will remember.

Avery wasn't always this way. There was a great light about her during her first three years but then life changed. Darkness covers skies and cities and, when we least expect it, on the most ordinary day, it can cover our lives. That's what Jennifer has learned.

"If we are people who pray," Jennifer's mother, Louise, said. "Then it's darkness that we often pray about."

She said that last week as she helped Jen clean her home. Louise has only a high school diploma and has worked for the last twenty-five years as an administrative assistant but is the wisest woman Jennifer knows. Jen hasn't always seen her mother this way but when she had Avery, her mother somehow became profoundly wise. Louise is quiet and never interfered in Jen and Michael's marriage, but she has always known when her daughter is weary or stressed or swallowed up in shadows.

"And what if we are people who can't pray?" Jennifer asked.

Louise thought for a moment. "Then it must be that darkness has stopped us." Jen fell into the sofa as a tear slipped onto her lap. Her mother sat next to her and pulled her close. "Things will get brighter, my love."

"When, Mom?" Jen wiped the wetness away. "When will it ever get brighter?"

Her mom shook her head. "I don't know. I don't know how many sunrises it will take but one day the sun will rise and you'll see that light still makes its way through. Even in the dark places."

Jennifer pulls into a parking spot at the front of the building and looks over her shoulder at Avery. "All set?" The little girl nods and unlatches her seat belt, sliding over and opening the door, leaving the angel on the seat. She holds Jennifer's hand and walks into Dr. Sondra Becke's office.

"Hi, Avery!" Rose says, looking up over the receptionist desk. "Would you like some juice or water while you wait?"

Avery sits on the floor and reaches for the toys that Dr. Becke keeps for her youngest patients. "No, thanks. I'm fine."

Rose smiles and looks at Jennifer. "It should only be a few minutes. She's finishing up with someone."

Jen sits on a chair by the window and reaches for a magazine she's already read. When she and Michael got married, Jennifer never imagined sitting in an office like Dr. Becke's but here she is. She's been bringing Avery here since just before last Christmas, when her troubles began. She glances up as a woman in her forties slips a credit card to Rose. In the beginning, Jennifer often wondered what was wrong with the person sitting across from her in the waiting room or exiting as she and Avery entered. Were they on the verge of divorce or fighting depression? She no longer wonders because she now knows what each of them wants. They want to know, just like her mom said, that light does make its way through the dark places.

"Hi, Avery!" Jennifer looks up to see Dr. Becke, crouching down next to Avery. Although she looks as if she's in her fifties,

Dr. Becke has the vitality of someone half her age. She keeps her bobbed hair colored a soft shade of brown with blond highlights and often wears a simple, white button-down shirt with trousers. "How many could you stack today?" she asks, looking at the tower of colorful blocks that Avery has erected.

"Only seventeen and then it smashed."

Dr. Becke stands with her hands on her hips. "That's great!"

"Not really," Avery says, throwing the blocks back into their plastic tub. "My record is twenty-four."

Dr. Becke holds out her hand for Avery. "Next time," she says, meaning it. Jennifer stands and follows them into Dr. Becke's office. It's warm in green and brown tones with soft, overstuffed furniture that Avery loves. She reaches for a stuffed animal on the back of the couch, a tiger she has named Homer, and clutches him to her chest as she settles into the cushions. "It's been three weeks," Dr. Becke says, without regarding her notes. "The last time we got together you had a fall festival at school." She sits next to Avery and leans toward her, tapping her leg. "How's first grade going?"

"Good," Avery says, bending Homer's ears up and down.

"What's your favorite part about it?"

Avery lifts her shoulders and scrunches up her face. "I like my teacher and I really like when we write stories on the computer."

Dr. Becke tilts her head back on the sofa and looks up at the ceiling. While Jennifer always feels uncomfortable and on edge when she first walks into her office, Dr. Becke eventually puts her at ease. "Stories on the computer! Can you tell me about one you're working on?"

"It's about a dog named Homer."

Dr. Becke leans up, her eyes widening. "Homer? I'm sensing a theme here," she says, squishing Homer under her hand. Avery giggles and relaxes farther into the cushions. "What is happening to Homer the dog?"

"He was outside playing with his brothers and sisters when he chased a rabbit but the rabbit wouldn't stop running and he ran all the way to a street where nobody knows him."

Dr. Becke snaps her head to look at Avery. "And?"

"And that's all."

Dr. Becke slaps her thighs. "That's all? Homer's on a street where nobody knows him and you just leave him there?"

Avery laughs and bounces the tiger on her

legs. "I still have to work on it."

"I should say so! You need to get Homer off that street and back with his family toot sweet! Do you know what that means?" Avery shakes her head. "It means fast! You can't leave Homer on some strange street with wayward rabbits and naughty cats. And don't get me started on all those misbehaving dogs!"

Avery smiles, shaking her head. "Maybe you should write the rest of it."

Dr. Becke and Jennifer laugh. "No! It's your story. And I want to read it when you're finished, okay?" Avery nods. Dr. Becke looks at Jen, raising her eyebrows. "So how are things?"

When Avery isn't looking, Jennifer raises her left hand and points to the ring. Dr. Becke nods. "Sleep is interrupted throughout the night," Jen says, nodding her head toward Avery. "And bed-wetting has started again."

Dr. Becke looks through her notes. "That started happening around this time last year."

Jen nods. "Then around February she just stopped. But now she's —"

Dr. Becke tugs on Homer's ear. "Are you waking up a lot?" Avery nods. "Is it a dream that's waking you?" The little girl shrugs.

"When you wake up can you remember seeing a face or any images?"

"I don't remember. I just wake up. A lot of times I wake up because the sheets are wet and I'm cold."

"Thankfully, sheets are easy to wash. Now if that was Homer, it'd be a different story! Tigers pee a lot!" Avery looks at her. "It's true! That's why it's a good idea to keep Homer here . . . so he won't pee in your bed."

Jennifer smiles and listens as Dr. Becke continues to draw words or feelings out of Avery. If darkness implies a world where nothing is seen very well — no clear answers or person or where she's going or even where she is now, then Jen knows more than she wants to know about it. If it suggests a sense of uncertainty or of feeling lost and afraid, then she's an expert. Each time she's in this office, she hopes for just a little light to walk out with.

"I'll see you next week," Dr. Becke says, touching her arm on the way out.

"And what about my wedding ring?" Jen whispers, holding up her hand.

Dr. Becke smiles. "It comforts her. You and Michael aren't divorced. She knows that. It might help her get through this bed-wetting episode."

Jennifer can remember those first three years with Avery when her mouth would spread wide in happiness on seeing her or Michael. She knows that kind of gladness exists in Avery; she just has to find a way to unlock it again, that's all.

Avery is quiet on the drive home. Although Jen points out the Christmas decorations on Grandon's town square and at the gazebo, Avery barely smiles. There was a time when she couldn't wait to hang the bulbs and ornaments on the Christmas tree and neither Jennifer nor Michael could even suggest that one of them place the angel on top! It's been a full week since Thanksgiving and Avery hasn't mentioned decorating a tree. Truth is, Jennifer doesn't feel like it, either, but knows she has to. "We should stop at the Christmas tree lot," she says, looking at Avery in the rearview mirror. "We could bring it home and make a day of it tomorrow!"

"I don't want to," Avery says, looking out the window.

Jennifer sighs, careful to keep her disappointment from showing. "I don't really want to, either, but it never really feels like Christmas without one."

Avery keeps her eyes on the passing buildings. "It doesn't feel like Christmas without Dad."

Jennifer takes a breath, wondering why Avery never says this sort of thing to Dr. Becke. Six months ago she got up on a bright summer day, walked to Jennifer's bedside and said, "Dads aren't supposed to leave."

People struggle every day to find a new normal. Jennifer knows that. She tires of people telling her that children are resilient or that they bounce back faster than adults from adverse circumstances. People who say that have never been with a child who's struggling to find a new way to do life. Jennifer had hoped the revelation was a breakthrough for Avery and that she would break into tears but she simply plopped down on the bed and turned on the TV.

"There's a Christmas tree lot just another mile or so down this road."

Avery looks at the back of her mother's head. "I don't want to decorate a Christmas tree. If that's your thing, then you do it."

Jennifer catches her eye in the mirror and wonders how a six-year-old can sound so grown-up. "It needs to be our thing together." Jennifer tries her best to sound cheery and confident but she knows that neither she nor Avery wants to do this.

Elhart Trees sets up residence at the far end of the strip mall each year. She can see the red banner from the stoplight. As she pulls into the parking lot she hears Avery sigh behind her. She gets out and opens the back door. "I already see one that looks like it could be perfect."

"Then you go get it and I'll wait here."

Jennifer winces. She can never outsmart her daughter.

"Looking for a tree?" Jennifer turns to see a man in his sixties wearing blue jeans, a red flannel shirt, and a Carhartt jacket. "I only cut down the sturdiest and prettiest trees I grow."

"If they're so pretty then why do you cut them down?" Avery asks from inside the car.

He leans over to look at her. "Because I can't keep all that pretty on my property. That'd be selfish. Just like if you stayed home and nobody ever saw you." Jennifer smiles and reaches for Avery's hand. "You just come get me or my grandson over there and we'll strap the tree to your roof."

"I don't want to decorate the tree," Avery says. "It's Mom's idea."

Mr. Elhart nods. "I see! You know, you would be amazed at how many people come here and tell me they are just not in the mood to decorate a Christmas tree. But do you know what happens when they have all the decorations on and they plug the lights in the first time?" Avery shakes her head. "That bad mood just disappears. It's like a magic trick! Did you know that it has been scientifically proven that you cannot sit in a room with a beautifully decorated Christmas tree and sip on a cup of hot cocoa and be in a bad mood?" Jennifer grins, listening.

"That's not true," Avery says.

The farmer shrugs. "I'm just telling you what I've read but you go home and try it and let me know."

To appease her mother and to get this over with as soon as possible, Avery marches to a tree roughly the same height as her mom and points to it. "I like this one."

"So do I!" It doesn't matter if Avery is rushing through the selection process; Jen's just glad that for a moment she's shown a little interest.

Mr. Elhart and his grandson strap it to the top of the roof and Mr. Elhart opens the door for Avery. "Still in a bad mood?" Avery nods. He brushes his hands off and whisks a few pine needles from his jacket. "I wish some of those scientists could be at your house in the next few days so that they could study you and write down the effects of decorating a Christmas tree."

"Why?"

"Because I know that Christmas trees always make things brighter. If they didn't, I may as well be growing something else."

He closes the door and Jennifer thanks him, hoping that he's right. It may not be a happy or glorious time, but for a moment or two, she's hoping the shadow of unbelief and sadness will fade, if even just a bit. Maybe neither one of them will manage to believe with all their hearts but she hopes that Avery will see that she and her mom and Christmas are most worth believing in.

Two

Arrange whatever pieces come your way.
— VIRGINIA WOOLF

Ryan Mazyck loads six-year-old Sofia's suitcase and his duffel bag into the backseat of the truck, holding the door open. "Hop in." He watches as she climbs into her booster seat and latches the seat belt.

"How long is this trip again?"

He slides behind the wheel and turns the key. "Just a couple of hours. Remember? We've been to visit Aunt Gloria and her husband, Marshall. It's the length of one movie or four TV episodes. So do you want to watch four *Jake and the Never Land Pirates* or *Frozen*?"

"*Frozen!*" She hands a DVD case to him. "Put it in please."

Ryan inserts the DVD and looks at her over his shoulder. "Put your headphones on."

"Why? Don't you want to sing along with me?"

Her face is so sincere that it makes him laugh. "Sure! I don't know what I was thinking."

Ryan hadn't expected this life ten years ago when he and Julie walked down the aisle. They had met in college in a business marketing class. She was petite and blond and laughed out loud at his jokes. When he looks in the rearview mirror he sees a tiny version of Julie. He has made this trip to Grandon only a handful of times in the last three years. Despite his best intentions, a lack of time and too much busyness have made the visits infrequent, but each time he travels this same familiar road, he remembers.

Three years ago he had been helping Gloria and Marshall with a simple bathroom redo. He told her the work she needed done would take no more than a couple of days, so he spent Saturday and most of Sunday with her and Marshall. He knew three-year-old Sofia would be sleeping when he arrived home that night after his two-hour trip but he would lean down and squeeze her just the same. He also knew that he and Julie would sit up talking into the night, catching up.

When he arrived home, the house was dark, except for a soft light in the living room. He walked through the kitchen and found Julie sitting in the living room on the swivel chair, the one they had found at a garage sale and had reupholstered. She was fully dressed and wearing her coat. "Did you just get home?" Ryan asked.

"No. I was just leaving."

She wasn't looking at him and Ryan stepped farther into the living room. "Just leaving? It's ten o'clock. Where are you going?"

She looked up at him and her eyes were a hard blue. "I thought you would be home sooner."

Ryan stood in front of her, looking around. "What's going on, Julie?"

She rubbed her palms along her thighs and lifted her shoulders as if she was shrugging. "I'm not happy, Ryan. I haven't been for a long time."

He felt his breath choking him and sat on the sofa. His heart struggled to beat and his voice lodged at the back of his throat. "What? Where's Sofia?"

"She's in her bed sleeping. I was going to take her with me but it got so late that she fell asleep, so I took her to bed." She wasn't looking at him again and Ryan wanted to take hold of her head and make her face him. "I've met someone. I didn't mean to. It just happened. He makes me happy. It's kind of ironic how the whole thing happened."

Ryan felt a laugh coming from somewhere deep within his chest and it surprised him, being louder than he anticipated. "Ironic? That's the word you choose for meeting another man and leaving me?"

Julie stood and walked to the front door. "Maybe it's for the best that Sofia fell asleep early tonight. That way she can be here with her bed and the things she loves, for the time being."

"You are one of those things that she loves, Julie."

She looked at him and the silence was heavy and perturbing between them. "We can work out custody later." She left him sitting alone in the living room. He stayed there all night.

He and Julie shared custody of Sofia for the next year but Julie's new life was taking her in a new direction. She married Derek and became stepmother to his three children. When Derek got a promotion, which meant a move to Arizona, Julie wanted to take Sofia with them. Ryan felt his world crumbling. "Don't make this situation ugly,

Ryan," Julie had said in the attorney's office.

Ryan never raised his voice, shook his finger, or banged on the table. Instead he whispered, "This is Sofia's life. I don't think of it as ugly but it would be devastating if she lived in Arizona. You know I'm a good dad, Julie. You know I have always worked hard for this family. You know I would do anything for her. Don't take her away from me. Please. She loves the house and her room and her dog."

Julie relinquished primary custody, and in ways that Ryan still thinks of as miraculous, they worked out a plan where Sofia would be with her mother several times a year. In the past three years, Ryan has stopped questioning the signals that he missed or the circumstances in which he failed her as a husband. It wasn't what he wanted or the life that he had planned but when he listens to the little voice behind him belting out the songs from *Frozen,* he knows he'd do it all over again.

"Are we finally here?" Sofia asks.

"We are here! This is Grandon."

She looks out the window. "This is where we're going to live now?"

He lifts his shoulders. "Maybe. It depends on which job I take. The job with Hazelton

Construction will be thirty minutes away, so we could either live here or closer to work. But if I take the job with Anderson Construction, that would mean we'd need to move to Riverside, four hours from here. I guess it all depends."

"Depends on what?"

"On what we discover in the next couple of weeks."

He drives around the town square, stretching glittery white in every direction, and hopes his and Sofia's future will be as bright as the snow around them.

"There," Jen says, placing a magenta-colored bulb with a velvet ribbon around it on the tree. Elvis's "Santa Bring My Baby Back (to Me)" can be heard from the portable CD player. Jen chose this compilation disc specifically for this song and others, thinking they would make Avery smile, but she hasn't paid attention. "It's really looking beautiful, isn't it?" Avery is holding a golden bulb and blown-glass snowman in her hands, looking at them. "Just find a spot anywhere, sweetie."

Avery looks up at her mom. "Why are we doing this, Mom? We aren't going to have any presents."

"Since when? Why wouldn't we?"

She talks into the bulb, turning it in her hands. "Naughty people don't get presents."

Jennifer reaches for another ornament, putting a hook on it. "You're thinking of Santa's naughty and nice list but there is no way you would be on the naughty list."

Avery hangs the snowman. "We're both on it."

Jen laughs. "What? How did we end up on the naughty list? We pay our taxes, we obey the law, we don't go around making life difficult for other people. Just this morning, I took Mrs. Lenox's mail to her that was accidentally put in our box. Most people would throw away her mail just so they wouldn't have to knock on her door, but I marched right up there and knocked on it and smiled as I handed her her mail. No one who faces Mrs. Lenox ends up on the naughty list."

"It's not the naughty list, Mom. It's the bad one."

Jen stops her work and looks at Avery. Elvis is annoying in the background. "What do you mean, Avery?"

She's holding a small reindeer ornament so tight that Jen fears she will crush it. "Dad isn't here."

Jennifer kneels down, tucking her legs under her. She reaches for Avery and pulls her down in front of her. "Dad's not being here has nothing to do with you or me."

Avery's face is like an art museum, with its most shining and beautiful works covered in canvas. "Yes it does."

Jen shakes her head, holding Avery's arms. "No. Listen to me. That's not how it works. None of this is your fault. None of this is my fault."

"He went away." Her eyes are about to spill over.

"But not because he chose to."

"God did it."

Jennifer's throat is swelling and she clears it. "We're not being punished. You're not being punished. Look at this." She's pointing to the tree and the ornaments. "This is Christmas. It's not punishment." Avery is shaking her head. "You are not bad. I'm not bad."

"Then why does it feel that way?"

Jen pulls her close, squeezing her tight. "I don't know, VV," she says, using the name Avery called herself as a toddler. "I don't know. But I'm going to do everything possible to help you *not* feel that way."

THREE

Where I am, I don't know. I'll never know, in the silence you don't know, you must go on, I can't go on, I'll go on.

— SAMUEL BECKETT

Gloria Wilson and Miriam Lloyd Davies pull in front of the Grandon Community Church and park. It's an old building, older than Gloria and Miriam combined, with a straight, white steeple, polished wood floors, and tall windows through which the light of God is slanting onto the communion table. The women are a study in contrasts. Miriam is a picture of English refinement, moving with elegance, like a high-masted sailboat, and never letting her features fall out of tune over the years. Gloria is a Georgia peach, with salt-and-pepper curls that bounce on her forehead as she takes off her coat and throws it on the front seat of the car. She's wearing red pants and a green reindeer sweatshirt with ornaments dangling from its antlers.

Miriam stares at her. "It's a wonder that Marshall let you out of the house. You look like a gaudy, tropical Christmas bird."

Gloria looks down at herself. "I hadn't thought of that. Thank you."

They walk up the stairs and Miriam swings open the door, mumbling, "It wasn't a compliment." She sighs, glancing around the empty lobby, and what looks like a curl forms on her upper lip. "What is it about churches? Why do they always have paintings or signs that say things like 'Believe in the Impossible' or 'Faith Can Move Mountains' or 'Hope Changes Everything'?"

Gloria jerks her head to look at her. "What do you want them to say? 'Give Up and Die'? It's a church!"

Miriam stops, finding the perfect spot inside her purse for the car keys. "I'm just saying, Gloria, that I'm quite sure God has good taste." Gloria rolls her eyes and Miriam leans closer to hear her. "What did you say? I hate it when you mumble."

"I said I hope you keep your big mouth shut during this meeting."

"That's a fine thing to say to someone, Gloria! You're like a big, heaving bull. It's a wonder all of your children aren't in therapy. You are no longer my best friend."

Gloria laughs, slapping Miriam on the arm. "You just said that two weeks ago."

Miriam pushes Gloria's hand away. "Well, I mean it this time!"

Years ago, the women had lived next to each other as strangers. Gloria had hoped that because they were both widows, they would have common ground, but Miriam was never interested in driveway conversations. Over ten years ago, faulty plumbing finally brought them together. Miriam used the toilet in her home before loading her bags in the car for a five-day trip. On returning, she was well rested but her home was waterlogged. Five days of running water destroys floors, walls, furniture, and makes for a very cranky neighbor. Gloria offered Miriam a bedroom in her home as Miriam's house was restored, and out of that rocky place a friendship bloomed. "It is a miracle!" Miriam often says of the friendship.

Together, they walk through the hallway and into Lily's office. "Oh! Didn't you get my message?" Lily asks.

"What message?" Gloria asks, sitting on one of the chairs opposite Lily's desk.

"I spoke with Marshall this morning and —"

Gloria waves her hands in the air. "That explains it! While Marshall has many great qualities, delivering messages is not one of them. What's happening, babe?"

"I let everyone know that the meeting was canceled because Linda's mother is in the hospital in critical condition. She's been dealing with dementia for the last couple of years and fell down the stairs in her home. One of her hips and the opposite leg is broken. Linda flew out this morning."

Miriam leans back and closes her eyes, shuddering. "Oh, that makes me hurt just thinking about it!"

"What does that mean for the Nativity?" Gloria asks.

"Well, Linda can no longer lead it so I need to find someone else." Lily rises and moves to the front of her desk, sitting on the edge. "And now that you're here I can ask you in person what I was going to call you about later."

"Oh, no! I've never been any less perfect for anything," Miriam says.

Gloria nods. "I rarely agree with her but she's right about this. And I'm afraid I wouldn't be any better."

Lily laughs and reaches for her coffee.

"Come on, Gloria! My father always says he would've scooped you up just like that to work in his law firm," she says, snapping her fingers.

"If Robert needed someone to bake a cake for the office, then I suppose I would have been the gal for the job." Gloria and Robert Layton have been longtime friends. He has offered his law services for several of the single moms at Glory's Place, the center for single moms and struggling families that Gloria opened years ago. Over the years, he and Kate have volunteered many times.

Although Lily teased her father about becoming a lawyer herself, she chose social services instead, working first for the local food bank when she and Stephen moved to Grandon and, for the last three years, as director of ministry services for Grandon Community Church. Lily is the one and only blonde of the family but she has Kate's warm eyes and Robert's smile. At thirty-five, she still looks as if she's in her twenties. "It just makes sense," Lily continues. "You're already on the team. All we need are costumes, a cast, a choir that is made up of adults and children, and a set. You don't need to do all of it, but is there anything you're good at on that list that you might be interested in? Anything would be helpful."

Miriam raises a finger in the air. "Actually, I studied acting in college and continued for several years after my husband and I married. He was also an actor. A bad actor but that's beside the point and it had nothing to do with our divorce." Gloria sighs and shakes her head, listening. "I do believe I could whip up a fine cast of characters for this Nativity. Do we need the usual lineup? Mary? Joseph? A ragamuffin group of shepherds and stately foreign visitors?"

"How about Jesus?" Gloria asks.

Miriam puts her hand up to hush her. "I know, Gloria! He is the star player. I'm not a loony bird."

"I think that has been tested and proven otherwise throughout the years." Gloria crosses her arms and leans back into the sofa. "All right, let me see. I could probably be useful working on costumes."

"Probably?" Miriam says. "She actually makes her own dishtowels! Who makes dishtowels? I have been given some of the tackiest dishtowels you have ever seen. If she can't make the costumes then no one can. The first century wasn't the peak of high fashion."

"You know," Gloria says. "My nephew

Ryan and his daughter will be staying with Marshall and me for two weeks. He's a contractor and is wanted by two companies, one not too far from Grandon. He has custody of his little girl, Sofia." She leans forward, whispering. "He's gone through a horrible divorce with his wife. She up and left him, taking just about everything, including the crockpot."

Miriam sounds as if she's breathing fire. "Oh, for the love of Pete! Would you please give up that crockpot!"

Gloria throws her hands into the air. "Why would she take the crockpot? The woman never cooked a day in her life. I say in any divorce each person should take the gifts that their own extended family members gave to them." She crosses her arms and looks at Lily as if everything she is saying makes perfect sense.

"You did not give them a deed to property or a home, for crying out loud! It was a forty-dollar crockpot."

Gloria shrugs. "All the same. I'm just saying it was rude." She looks at Lily. "While Sofia is on Christmas break, Ryan is going to be looking for a place to live in case he takes the job that's just thirty minutes from here. I'm sure I could talk him into helping with the sets."

"Oh, sure!" Miriam says. "What young man from out of town wouldn't love to help put together a church Nativity?"

Gloria waves her hand in front of Miriam's face. "You of little faith. You do not have because you do not ask! You should have a sign hanging in your home that says, 'Life . . . eh . . . Whatever'."

Lily laughs and sits at her desk, reaching for a pen and sticky note. "Miriam, I'll write some names of people who have been in the Nativity in previous years. Craig Grant has been Joseph a couple of times and might do it again." She writes several more names before handing the note to Miriam. "Jamie Ledsom has been Mary, so who knows? She may also like to take part in this again."

Miriam reaches for the note and slips it into her purse. "Jamie Ledsom, who has just had her fourth child and is in her late thirties? Thank you but I already have some wonderful ideas about how to find the perfect cast."

Gloria reaches for her purse and puts it on her lap. "I need to get home and start making lunch."

Miriam raises her arms as if someone has just made a touchdown. "That's it! She's hungry so we may as well shut down. She's like a rumbling freight train when she gets hungry so there's no point in trying to focus any longer."

Gloria turns to her in a huff. "I am tired of being compared to a bull and a freight train!"

Lily leans onto her desk, watching them leave. "You both will be awesome."

Gloria laughs, stopping at the door. "I don't know about awesome but I'm sure we'll bring new meaning to working with cracked pots."

As he drives past the front of the elementary school, Ryan realizes he has taken the wrong turn but looks over his shoulder at Sofia, pointing. "If we live in Grandon and we bought the house that we looked at this morning, the one with the big backyard, you would go to this school."

Sofia looks up and stretches her neck for a better angle. "Let's go in there, Dad."

"But there is nothing for us to do yet. I mean, we don't even know if we'll end up in Grandon or in Riverside."

"Then this might help us decide. This might be such an awesome school that you won't even want to think about that other job. We already know we like the house with the big backyard, right? Why do we have to move four hours away?"

"Because I might be better suited for the job in Riverside. That's why I'm talking to both companies and interviewing with them."

"Come on, Dad. Let's just look at it. What will it hurt? That's what you always say, right?"

He thinks it is a waste of time this early in their search but he nods, saying, "Yep! That's what I always say." In the school office, two women are behind the long countertop: an older woman sitting at a desk, wearing an elf's hat and talking on the phone, and another, younger woman, wearing a tall Cat in the Hat hat, is sifting through a file folder. "Are you signing her back in?" Ryan realizes the young woman is talking to him but doesn't answer fast enough. "Did you sign her out to go to the doctor or is she just coming in for the day?" When she smiles, Ryan is glad he made the wrong turn and ended up here in the office looking at her. Since Julie left he has come to believe that what happens to people isn't just by accident, like the scattering of leaves in the wind, but that there is a divine order to life and that situations and events and wrong turns don't just lead anywhere but to the somewhere we are supposed to be.

"No, Sofia's not a student. We're looking

at possibly living in the area and Sofia wanted to check out the school."

The woman glances over her shoulder at the older woman, who is still on the phone. "Barb is actually the office manager and can find all the information that you need. I work in the kindergarten hall and don't know my way around Barb's files."

"That's okay. We can wait. I'm Ryan and this is Sofia."

"I'm Jen. I have a daughter in first grade here and as a parent and an employee I can say that it's a great school." Her eyes are a combination of blue and fine ash and Ryan realizes he has rarely noticed a woman's eyes in the last three years. When Barb hangs up the phone and gets to her feet, Jen turns toward the door. "I hope you find something soon that your family loves and, Sofia, I hope I'll be seeing you in the halls." That's just what Ryan was hoping, too.

Jennifer helps put folders and lunchboxes into backpacks before the children line up at the sound of the bell. She has been working as a kindergarten aide for the last two years; this year she's in Mrs. Cranston's room. She loves the work because it enables her and Avery to stay on the same schedule. They get up together, ride to school together, and come home at the end of the day. Jen often catches glimpses of Avery inside her own classroom and in the cafeteria and a sharp ache fills her chest. She looks for brightness but only sees deep shadows. Avery reminds Jen of winter, when every bulb or bloom seems choked, but she hopes that her little girl, like the flowers in spring, will lift her head and stretch toward the sun.

While she waits for Avery, Jen checks her voice mail. Dr. Plantiga's office has returned her call and she dials the number again. "Hi, this is Jennifer De Luca. Marianne returned my call today. Could I talk to her about setting up an appointment with Dr. Plantiga?"

"Let me transfer you," the woman says on the other end.

Jennifer sighs when her call goes to voice mail. She has called two doctors and has gotten no further than voice mail each time. "This is Jennifer De Luca. You returned my call today about my husband, Michael. I'm wondering if I can set up an appointment with Dr. Plantiga? Just call me back at your convenience. Thank you." She hangs up as Avery walks into Mrs. Cranston's classroom. "Hi, VV! How was your day?"

"Good. Do we have to go anywhere after

45

school, Mom?"

Jennifer knows she's asking about going to see Dr. Becke. Although Dr. Becke is always very kind and Avery is comfortable with her, Jen knows she'd rather whisper her secrets under starlight than in an office. "Not today, but we will be going to see Dr. Becke later this week. I do need to run to the grocery, though."

Avery slings her backpack over her shoulders and grabs her mother's hand. "What are we having for dinner?"

They walk into the hall and join the many lines of children walking to their bus exit, car pickup line, or afterschool program. "That's what we need to decide and why I have to go to the store!"

"How about chicken and biscuits?"

Jennifer smiles. "I think that's possible. I'll just have to buy one of those chickens that's already been cooked back in the deli section. Otherwise, it would take half the night cooking the chicken and getting the rest prepared."

Avery opens the back door of the car. "Well, it is Dad's favorite, you know?"

Jennifer laughs. "Yes, I've been told that a few hundred times."

As Jennifer points to each item on the shelves Avery puts it into the shopping cart.

They make their way through the produce, meat, and dairy sections before standing in line at the deli. Avery is deciding which sandwich meat she wants as Jen picks out a roasted chicken.

"Jennifer?"

She turns to see Miriam, dressed in a long black coat and bright red scarf. There has always been a golden hue of sorts around Miriam, who looks more like a film star from the 1960s than a resident of Grandon. She sets the chicken in her cart and gives Miriam a hug. "How are you?"

"Very well. We've missed you down at Glory's Place."

Jen sighs. "Time has gotten away from me," she says, glancing at Avery. "We have the best intentions of coming back."

Miriam smiles. "And we will gladly welcome you back. Any time." She leans down and looks at Avery. "You are stunningly beautiful. Do you know that?" Avery looks at her mother and then runs her fingers along the top of the cart. Miriam laughs. "Oh, the broken hearts over this one," she says, smiling at Jen.

"How is everyone at Glory's Place? How is Miss Glory? Dalton and Heddy?"

Miriam rolls her eyes at the sound of "Miss Glory." When she and Gloria first met, Miriam told her that Miss Glory was not the name for a grown woman. "Gloria is a tragic yet comical figure, as always. And Dalton and Heddy are well on the way to sainthood for working with her all these years." She slaps the handle of the cart and cocks her head, looking at Jennifer. "Gloria and I are actually heading up the Nativity at the church. I have been given the task of finding children for the angel choir and casting the roles." She looks at Avery and back to Jennifer, smiling. "Do you think Avery would be interested in singing with the angel choir? It's not just children. There will be adults singing, too." Jennifer catches Avery's eyes and begins to speak but Miriam isn't finished. She leans down to Avery. "Your beautiful red hair would fill that church with vibrant color! And your voice, joined with all the other children's voices, would float through those doors straight up to heaven."

Jen covers her mouth to keep from smiling. Avery looks up at her, uncertain of Miriam's stability and unsure of what she's asking. "Thank you for thinking of her, Miriam, but I can't sing and I don't know if Avery —"

"But I do know! She would be wonderful. And she would be part of something truly beautiful and touching at Christmas. Surely no one could say no to such an experience. As Gloria always says, 'No one can deny the many miracles of Christmas.' " She groans. "Now I've done it! I have quoted Gloria. I have no idea what that implies but it frightens me." She shakes her head, indicating there is no time to think about that right now. "Please join us. It will do all of us a world of good."

Jennifer lifts her eyebrows. Somehow, Gloria and Miriam have always had a way with persuasion, and there is a part of her that wants to believe that Avery could be part of the miracles at Christmastime. "But we don't go to that church and —"

"It doesn't matter," Miriam says, nearly bursting with enthusiasm. "They let me in a long time ago so that just proves they have an open-door policy." She inhales as if to take half of the deli with her and nods, smiling. "I will call you soon and let you know when practice begins." And as an afterthought says, "We will need help with other things, too. I mean, since you can't sing but will be driving Avery to practice. Perhaps you would like to help Gloria with costumes. No pressure. Just throwing it out there since you'll be sitting around and waiting for Avery anyway."

Jennifer shakes her head, laughing. "I'll think about it."

Miriam claps her hands together and then grabs her cart, pushing it away. "Oh, what fun we'll have! I'll be in touch soon."

Avery looks at her mom and frowns. "What did you just do?"

Jennifer isn't sure but she's hoping this Nativity will be the little bit of light that she's been looking for.

FOUR

There are two ways of spreading light: to be the candle or the mirror that reflects it.
— EDITH WHARTON

Miriam notices the Christmas tree lot where it has stood for the last umpteen dozen years and, on a whim, pulls in. She's had the same artificial tree for the last ten years and decides right now, at this moment, that she wants a real one.

"I've got lots of Fraser firs. Any size you want," Mr. Elhart says, waving his arm.

Miriam nods and walks through the rows of trees, touching their branches. A teenage girl with her mother can be overheard arguing and Miriam moves closer, practicing her gift of eavesdropping. "This is the last Christmas we'll have together as this family," the mother says. "All I'm asking for is a little interest and participation."

"I didn't need to help you do this," the

teenager says. Miriam rolls her eyes, listening. Teenagers never want to help with anything.

"You didn't need to come but I *wanted* you to come. Everything will be different next year. We'll be in a new state. The family will be different. I just wanted one last . . ." Miriam strains to hear but the mother's voice has faded to a whisper. Miriam's mind races as she wonders what is happening in the family that will change it so drastically. She continues to browse through the trees, pretending not to listen, when the girl steps into her row. Her stomach has taken on an orbit of its own and Miriam understands why the mother has grown quiet. She feigns the greatest interest in each needle and branch of the tree in front of her as the girl passes behind her.

"When are you due?" Miriam hears herself asking.

The young girl looks at her, sizing her up before she answers. "The beginning of February."

"A New Year's baby! A new year, a new start, and a new life. How very exciting!" The girl tries to smile and her mother steps in beside her. Miriam smiles at her. "I'm Miriam Lloyd Davies. I help at Glory's Place."

The girl's mother nods. "Oh. I'm familiar with it."

"We love young mothers there," Miriam says. She looks at the girl. "And we love their children. My friend Gloria runs it and she's the closest thing to a saint I've ever seen but I will deny saying that if you ever tell her."

"Thank you," the mother says. "But we won't be here much longer. We'll be moving to Arizona in February. We had planned to move this month but then thought we should wait until Kaylee has the baby."

Miriam watches as Kaylee shrinks back, flinching at her mother's comment. In an uncharacteristic manner Miriam takes hold of the girl's hand and looks at her. Kaylee's eyes, drowned in the understanding of what is growing inside her, are glistening and pitiful. "This will be an extraordinary moment for everyone involved and the thought that God is always smirking and angry will be gone." Kaylee's mother notices the tears in her daughter's eyes and wraps her arm around her, pulling her close. Miriam releases the girl's hand and steps back, feeling out of place. "My very best to both of you." She begins to back away when words form inside her chest and gallop through her mouth as if they are stretching out their necks at the Preakness. "This is a crazy thought but I'm wondering if you've ever had any desire to be in a Nativity?"

"You asked a pregnant girl to be Mary?"

"Yes, Gloria! For a dozen times now . . . Yes! Yes, I did."

Gloria dries a bowl and hands it to Miriam. "Put it in that cabinet," she says, pointing with her head. "Do you know the story of the Nativity? Mary *gives* birth."

Miriam sighs, closing the cabinet on the bowl and taking a pot from Gloria. "But she was pregnant a whole lot longer than she was giving birth. I am so tired of seeing thirty-year-old Marys. She was a teenager. I saw a teenager and asked her."

Gloria dries a handful of forks and spoons and hands them to Miriam. "And she said yes?"

Miriam throws the silverware into the drawer. "Oh, no! Absolutely not." She closes the drawer and leans against the counter. "I don't know what it was but there was something about that girl. She and her mother were there arguing and the next thing I know I saw this huge pregnant belly and was holding her hand."

Gloria stops her work. "You held her hand?"

Miriam nods.

"Did she spontaneously combust?"

Miriam throws her head back and laughs. "I don't know what happened but when I looked at her I just felt something, and I'm —"

"Not prone to feelings?"

Miriam swats her with the dishtowel and shakes her head, waving her hand in the air as if it would make Gloria disappear.

Gloria sighs, also shaking her head, taking it in. "You reached out and held someone's hand. That whole situation is just one of the miracles of Christmas!"

Miriam reaches for a cup from the cupboard. "I knew you would say that. I even quoted you today to Jennifer De Luca and her daughter and to Ray Elhart, the Christmas tree farmer."

"Why did you quote me to the Christmas tree farmer?"

Miriam's eyes bug out as she looks at Gloria. "Because I told him he looked like a shepherd and if he chose to be a shepherd in the Nativity then he might possibly be part of one of the miracles of Christmas."

Gloria stops wiping the stovetop and squeezes her temples between her fingers. "You actually told a man he looked like a shepherd and that wasn't offensive to him?"

"Had you said it, yes, it would have been offensive, but from my mouth it sounded as if he was a king about to survey his kingdom."

Gloria laughs, scrubbing harder. "And he said yes?"

Miriam pours coffee into her cup and sits at the table. "No. I was zero for two at that Christmas tree lot. He lives twenty miles away on a farm, you know, with the trees and the cows. Not that that had anything to do with him saying no, but he is quite busy tending to the cows in addition to cutting down trees. He did say he would come to the Nativity because it just so happens he has provided a tree for the church's lobby for the last several years. Old hunting buddies with Pastor Bill. I did, however, find Joseph changing my oil today."

Gloria sits at the table. "There are so many places I could go with that but I won't!"

"You asked Ryan to help build the sets, didn't you?"

"Of course I did, and he said yes!" Gloria makes a grunting sound in the back of her throat and spins a napkin on the table in front of her. "That boy is like an empty room."

Miriam narrows her eyes and tilts her

head. "Is that one of your Georgia South-ernisms? Because I have no idea what you're talking about."

"He's like a dry twig hanging from a high branch."

Miriam shakes her head and raises a hand in the air. "Honestly, Gloria! How does Marshall understand you? Just speak English."

Gloria grins and swipes the napkin back and forth on the table. "He's lonely and I feel awful for him. When he married that woman he thought it was for keeps. He probably thought the crockpot was for keeps, too, but he was wrong on both counts."

Miriam presses her palms into her forehead and groans. "Again with the crockpot. Ryan is a good guy. Hard worker. Good dad. That can go a long way in this world."

The front door opens and Sofia stamps her boots on the rug as if stomping out a brush fire. "We were just talking about you!" Gloria says. "How was the first day of house hunting? Did Susan show you some nice homes?"

Sofia slings her coat to her father and steps inside the kitchen. "I liked one of them," she says, holding up a tiny finger. "It had three bedrooms, a big backyard, and a cool basement with black-and-white tile for playing in! I've never had a basement. Then we visited the school I'd go to and got to walk around. They have a computer lab and a big art room and a huge playground."

"It sounds perfect," Miriam says, winking at Ryan. "And how exciting is it knowing that you could be so close to your old aunt Gloria and her vibrant friend Miriam?" Gloria moans and Ryan smiles. "We were just talking about the Nativity before you walked in."

"You can call off the dogs, Miriam," Ryan says, pulling a glass from a cupboard and filling it with ice. "I already said I'd help."

Miriam smiles, watching Sofia. "I know that but I was thinking of Sofia. You know, you would be perfect for the angel choir."

"I can't sing," the little girl says, keeping her head tilted like a doll's.

"That's never stopped anyone before! Just turn on any radio station and listen for a few minutes," Miriam says. "You will be just the addition we're looking for and your old auntie Gloria here will be making an adorable costume for each one of you."

"I guess I could," Sofia says, looking at her dad.

Miriam claps her hands together and presses one cheek and then the other to

Sofia's, causing her to scrunch up her face. Gloria laughs, watching her. "You'll get used to her, Sofia. You'll find out that being around Miriam feels a lot like a sickness."

Ryan laughs, sitting down at the table and pulling Sofia onto his lap. His aunt and Miriam always make him feel as if something great and promising is about to happen, just beyond the next door. He is beginning to feel as if the biggest turning point in his life is less likely to be the day he walked down the aisle or when Sofia was born or even the day that Julie left him. The real turning point is more likely to be this one with its hope of new and opening doors.

FIVE

The best way out is always through.
— ROBERT FROST

The rain rattles on the window of Dr. Becke's office, the watery streams looking like waves and blisters in the glass. Jen watches as Avery draws and colors a picture of a balloon on the coffee table. Jen assumes that Dr. Becke would probably say the picture is a good sign; but Jen can't help but think that Avery's spirit is as deflated as a day-old balloon. Maybe that's what the picture represents instead.

"We had a conversation," Jen starts. "She somehow feels that her dad's not being here is her fault. My fault. That we are bad people and this is our punishment."

Dr. Becke nods, watching Avery draw. "You think that what happened is your —"

"I don't want to talk about what happened," Avery says. "I keep saying that."

"And I keep saying that we have to talk about it," Dr. Becke says, smiling.

"You two talk about it all the time," Avery says without glancing up. "Seems to me that's enough."

Dr. Becke looks at Jen and they both know that Avery can be pushed only so far. "How are you sleeping?"

Avery shrugs. She is cautious, as if observing herself from a distance. Giving away too much might let too many people in. "Good." Dr. Becke looks at Jennifer and she shakes her head. Avery's bed-wetting has not stopped.

"Do you dream about your dad while you sleep?"

Jennifer leans over, resting her forearms on her knees. For months her own sleep has been swept clean of dreams.

"Sometimes."

"And what is your dad doing in your dreams?"

Avery picks up a red crayon and begins coloring the balloon, shaking her head. "I don't know. I don't remember. I just see him and I tell him that dads don't leave." Jennifer's heart pitches to her throat and she looks at the rug under her feet.

Dr. Becke sits on the floor on the opposite side of the coffee table and reaches for a blank sheet of paper and some crayons. "Does he say anything to you?"

Avery picks another shade of red and adds deeper shades to the balloon. "Nope. He just leaves again."

"Are you sad when you see him?" Avery nods. "Are you afraid?" She shakes her head. "Do you feel frustrated or anxious in the dream?"

Avery adds a long tail to the balloon and begins to color a blue sky behind it. "I feel frustrated."

"Why?"

"Because I want to talk to him and can't. I always want to call him but Mom says . . ." She doesn't finish.

"Have you tried to call him?"

She nods, making huge strokes on the paper. "He won't answer the phone. There aren't any phones in heaven." Jennifer wipes a tear from her eye before Avery can see.

"What would you ask him?" Dr. Becke says.

Avery doesn't look up from her drawing. "I'd ask him why he left."

Jen looks up at the ceiling, hoping her tears will remain locked in place.

Dr. Becke leans forward. "And what do you want your dad to say?"

"I want him to say that he'll come back

home and play with me and make pancakes with Mom on Saturday morning." Avery fills in every trace of white on the paper and Jen wipes her face.

After several more questions about school and favorite things to do the session ends. Dr. Becke hangs the picture of the balloon over her desk and opens a drawer, filled with small packages of Goldfish crackers. Avery reaches for one and looks to her mother, who nods. She opens it and walks into the waiting room, sitting down next to the toys. Dr. Becke and Jennifer stand in the hallway where they can talk and still keep an eye on Avery. "She's not fearful," Dr. Becke says. "I see children who are afraid and Avery is not one of them."

"Then why is she wetting the bed again?" Jen whispers.

Dr. Becke crosses her arms, revealing short, plain, yet well-manicured nails. "Because the past caught up with her last year at this time and it's catching up with her again. It's actually a good thing. It has taken her a while but she's peeling back the layers of grief."

Jen watches her daughter as she has watched her so many times over the years, feeling as if any moment her chest would burst open. She would do anything to take away the wordless meals and the anxious nights of sleep. She would pay anything to hear Avery's laugh again. She feels the lump in her throat and remains quiet.

Dr. Becke smiles, touching her shoulder. "Keep talking. Keep encouraging her to try new things. And talk more at bedtime. Talk about rest for her mind and her body and the excitement of a new day tomorrow. Sunrise has a way of wiping the slate clean, bringing with it a new day."

Jennifer nods. A new day. They survived yesterday and the yesterdays before that and will awaken to a new day. But what about tomorrow? "Go where you are needed," her mother keeps saying. "Do what is needed. Take care of the needs of today and the rest will take care of itself." Jennifer is doing her part but she feels that "the rest" is not holding to its part of the bargain and she always finds herself hoping for more. She often wishes she could pick up the threads of yesterday, wad them together between her thumb and index finger, and throw them away. Each time they visit Dr. Becke's office she hopes for giant strides but comes away with yet another baby step to help Avery take.

When she made this appointment, Jen had no idea that they would be helping with the

Nativity. Avery's first practice is scheduled for immediately afterward, and although Jen feels emotionally drained, she is surprised when Avery doesn't complain about going. They follow the noise inside the church, past the lobby, and down the hall to the choir room. A couple dozen adults and children stand and sit among the chairs, talking. Gloria and Miriam are next to the piano, bent over the music. Their words come out like a fast-paced melody. Miriam is wearing a red angora sweater and white pearls and Gloria is in a red sweatshirt decorated with a snowman wearing a top hat. Jen smiles as she looks at them, and holding Avery's hand, she is filled with a quivering lurch of excitement for her.

"Well, look at you, babe!" Gloria's arms are open and moving toward her, drawing her in. "It has been several months, hasn't it?"

Jen smiles. "I told Miriam we have every intention of coming back to Glory's Place."

"Well, you know that Dalton and Heddy would be thrilled to see you there again and I would be over-the-moon excited." She laughs and bends over, looking at Avery. "When Miriam told me you were going to be part of the angel choir I just knew it was going to be the best choir ever!" She takes her hand and leads her away from Jennifer. "You can come right over here and sit down next to Sofia and Miss Lily. Miss Lily's responsible for Miriam and me being in charge of the Nativity this year, so if anything goes wrong, be sure to blame her." Lily pats the chair next to her and Avery sits and glances at her mom. Jen smiles, nodding.

Gloria races back to Jennifer's side, lacing an arm with hers. "Miriam said you would think about helping out. Have you?" Jen smiles and that's enough for Gloria. "I'm hoping that means yes!"

Jen throws her arms into the air. "Anything for you, Gloria!"

"And God," Gloria says.

"Of course! That's a given in His house and all."

Gloria laughs, squeezing her arm. "Do you think you could help my nephew with the set whenever he needs it and then give me some help with the costumes down the road?"

"Sure, Gloria. Wherever you need me is fine but I don't know anything about building a set."

"I have complete confidence in you," Gloria says, pointing. "Ryan's in the big room at the end of the hall. You can't miss it, it's the one with all the hammering going on."

Jen takes a final look at Avery, who seems engrossed in a polite conversation with Sofia and Lily. She doesn't hear hammering but pokes her head inside the door at the end of the hall. A large plywood wall has been erected in the center of the room and chairs have been stacked and moved against the walls.

"Hello! Is Ryan in here?"

Ryan looks around the plywood, stepping out in front of it. Jen laughs, shaking her head. "When Gloria said 'nephew,' I pictured a fifteen-year-old."

She is lovely, carved in soft lines with a smile a bit crooked and shy. Her dark hair is pulled back into a ponytail. Her jeans fit just so, and Ryan feels like his brain is a fluid, slippery mess inside his head. "I'm sure she probably still pictures me that way."

He steps closer and Jen feels a catch in her chest. His face has been weathered by hope and pain, and he has coffee-brown eyes and sandy hair.

"No Cat in the Hat hat today?" he asks.

The memory collapses Jennifer's face into a scowl and then she laughs. "What a way to be remembered! That was silly-hat day at school. I typically don't wear that hat in public."

"Do you save the cheese-head hat for that?"

Jen laughs and slides her purse strap farther up onto her shoulder. "I hope your family has decided where to live."

"We're still looking. I have a couple of job offers, so we could find something here in Grandon and that would give me a thirty-minute drive to Hazelton Construction, or if I take the job in Riverside, that'd be a move four hours away. So far, Sofia likes a house here but I'm still interviewing with both companies."

"What about your wife? What does she like?"

Ryan picks up his hammer and studies it. "It's just Sofia and me. I'm divorced."

Jen is often uncertain how to react to someone when they say they are divorced. Is *I'm sorry* appropriate? Or *Whew! I bet you're glad that's over!*

"It's funny but there are few people who tell you that marriage could be a bumpy and dangerous ride."

He nods. "Divorce is hard. So many times I thought it'd be so much easier if Julie just wasn't here. You know, it'd be easier if she'd passed away than deal with so much stuff that we keep dealing with." Ryan looks at her and realizes he's said too much. His eyes fall on her ring and something sharp slips beneath his skin.

This is one of those moments when Ryan could be swept along in a current of sadness, remembering what he once had and realizing there are some things he may never have again. He turns away so she can't see the look on his face. When he was growing up, Ryan's father always told him that if he wasn't paying attention, if he was looking the other way, a moment might come that he's been waiting for, and he'll miss it. But sometimes, Ryan knows, he can't look too hard or too long. He just has to turn away, hoping the moment will pass.

He's grateful when Ed and Gabrielle return. Ed is a grandpa and self-professed handyman. Within minutes of meeting him, Ryan knew he has four grandchildren, worked in the administrative offices of the local school system before retiring, and has been married for forty-three years. Gabrielle is single and in her late twenties. Her legs are long, her hair is soft, and her laugh is loud as she enters the room. "This is Ed Law and Gabrielle Marvin. They're helping, along with three others who aren't here yet. This is Jennifer."

She smiles. He had remembered her name.

"Are you part of the singles group?" Gabrielle asks. She is a fine-boned brunette with pale green eyes and a brow crinkled together in a girlish way as if something new and exciting is always on her mind.

Jennifer shakes her head. "No."

"I didn't think I'd ever seen you." She turns her attention to Ryan. "The group is putting together shoe boxes for Operation Christmas Child on Saturday. Maybe that's something you and Sofia would like to help with. Lots of kids will be there."

Ryan reaches into a box of nails and smiles at Gabrielle. "That'd be great."

Gabrielle smiles. Jen thinks she looks satisfied and as if she's on her way to something new. Jen has no reason to feel sad but she does.

"So, we are the stable makers," Ed says, lifting a piece of plywood. "Let's see your hands, young gal." Jen holds up her hands, smiling. "Eh, I guess they'll do. Check out that hand," he says, holding his palm in front of her. "Nice and big. Good for lifting, hammering, and such." He claps his hand against the board. "Well . . . let's start cobbling this thing together."

Jen takes off her jacket and lays it across a

chair. She's cobbling together new days for herself and Avery as best she can. Maybe the miracles of Christmas that Gloria talks about are somewhere there in the cobbling.

SIX

The quality of mercy is not strained;
It droppeth as the gentle rain from heaven
Upon the place beneath. It is twice blest;
It blesseth him that gives and him that
    takes . . .

              — WILLIAM SHAKESPEARE

Sixteen-year-old Kaylee stands on the sidewalk in front of the church, looking at it. Part of her wants to believe there is something inside those walls for someone like her, but the other part, the part that feels trashy and trashed, believes otherwise. Sex wasn't anything like what she has seen in the movies or on TV and scripted dialogue has never come close to her feelings of betrayal and loss after telling Jared she was pregnant. When word got out, it was obvious that she was considered the one who had been on the prowl for a quick hookup. The looks and murmurs among her classmates were reserved for her, not Jared. She was the slut, not him. For the last four months she has been homeschooled around her mother's work schedule.

She and Jared tried to make things work but an expanding belly gets in the way of football and homework and hanging with friends, and whatever relationship they had began to fizzle. Then there was the awkward conversation with her parents and Jared's parents about child support where Jared would never make eye contact with her and she knew it was over. Unlike television shows, there has been no witty or dramatic script with profound words of loneliness, anger, doubt, and shame for her to speak. She shoves her hands deep into her pockets and looks up at the church, Grandon Community. This is the one that the woman at the Christmas tree lot told her about. She has lived in Grandon all her life but has rarely noticed it; she and her parents went to another church, the one on the other side of town with the big gymnasium, at Christmas and sometimes Easter.

"Are you headed inside?" The voice is somewhere behind her. "Are you going in?" She turns to see a woman pulling grocery bags out of her car. "I have a couple more of these if you have a free hand."

"Sure." Kaylee walks to the back car door and pulls two bags from the seat.

"I'm Lily, by the way." Kaylee follows her up the stairs. "Are you here for practice?"

Kaylee follows her through the door. "No."

Lily leads her through the church and into a small kitchen and begins to pull out packages of water bottles, cutting away the plastic packaging and putting the bottles in the refrigerator. The young girl is pretty in a simple way with shoulder-length brown hair and colorless eyes. They are colorless but not in the sense that they are not brown or blue (because they are blue) but colorless in the sense that she doesn't seem to see the pinks of joy or the reds of hope or the yellows of laughter anymore. "Did you drop someone off?"

Kaylee hands her a few bottles of water. "No, I don't know anyone here."

Lily stops stocking the refrigerator and laughs. "I am so sorry! It looked like you were headed up the steps so I thought you were here for rehearsal. You must think I'm crazy!"

Kaylee hands her three more bottles of water. "No big deal. I was driving by."

Lily refrains from asking why she was standing in front of the church if she was just driving by because she thinks there's something wrung out about Kaylee's face, making it seem full of sadness. She reaches for another package of water bottles and notices Kaylee's belly for the first time. There it is again. That unnamed sadness spreading through her. "I shouldn't have assumed that you were coming here. Thanks so much for helping me, though. I'm glad you followed the nudge and decided to stand there." She closes the refrigerator door and hands Kaylee a bottle of water.

"What do you mean, I followed the nudge?"

Lily walks to the cabinets and stops. "You know how sometimes you take a street that you didn't plan on or you call a friend out of the blue? You don't really know why, you just kind of felt a nudge to go down that street or to text a friend. We get a lot of people who just kind of wander into the church and they can't really explain why. It's just a nudge, you know." She opens a cabinet and talks over her shoulder. "Sometimes, they come into the building just to sit."

"Why do they just sit?"

"Probably looking for a quiet place to think. Some of them may feel God is a little closer here. Lots of reasons, I guess." She stops her work and looks at Kaylee. "Do you live in the downtown area?"

Kaylee shakes her head. "No. I was just driving by."

Lily notices that she has said she was driving by again, but knows that Kaylee wasn't just driving around. She had driven to the church and gotten out of the car for some reason. She pulls out a box of tea and a box of cocoa, shaking them. "Interested?"

Kaylee points. "Cocoa. Thanks. A lady told me about the Nativity you're doing and when I got in front of the church I recognized the name."

Lily reaches for two mugs and fills them with water before setting them inside the microwave. "You should come. Bring your parents." Kaylee doesn't respond and an abrupt, releasing quiet settles on the room. "When are you due?" She takes the grocery bags off the table and wads them up, nodding at a chair. "Feel free to sit."

Kaylee leaves her coat on but sits at the table. "The beginning of February."

The microwave beeps and Lily removes the mugs, pouring the packets of cocoa inside. She worries about saying something dumb but can't avoid the elephant in the room. "Do you have any names picked out?"

"I don't know. I actually like Abby for a

girl and I haven't thought of a name for a boy yet."

"There's lots to choose from," Lily says, setting a mug in front of Kaylee. "Are you excited?"

Kaylee takes hold of the handle and stares into the mug. She doesn't answer and Lily groans inside. She has already said something dumb and now there is the danger of this young girl drifting away and never being seen again. She sits at the table and reaches out, patting the girl's arm. "You may not see it now but you'll be okay." Kaylee looks at her with watery blue eyes. "It might take a while. I hope it won't but it might. It won't be painless. I hope it is but it might not be. But you will be okay."

"How do you know?"

Lily shrugs. "Because I've seen it over and over. I've seen broken people who were held together by no more than a thread who are now okay. I've seen trapped people who are now free. I've seen hurt people who are now healthy. It took time for all of them but they are okay. Circumstances do change. Sometimes it just takes a long time to get there."

A tear makes its way down Kaylee's cheek and onto the table. "Have you seen stupid people who are okay?" Lily's eyes are brimming with hope, and another tear falls in front of Kaylee as she shakes her head.

"I've never seen stupid people," Lily says. "But I have seen people who have made mistakes who are now okay. My own dad made some choices many years ago that almost cost him his family: my mom, sister, and me. My mom was ready to leave because of his choices and he was ready to let us go but he didn't. It wasn't a good time for us but he's okay now and I think he's a great man. Things turn around."

"I hope you're right."

Her voice is so small that Lily has to lean in close to hear. "I am," Lily says.

Kaylee looks into her cocoa, searching for something. "My boyfriend doesn't want anything to do with me or the baby. I'm sure you were dying to know that."

Lily swirls the cocoa inside her mug. "I'm sorry. I can't imagine not being interested in a baby or in you."

"My parents hate me because of this."

Lily shakes her head. "No they don't. I'm sure they feel sadness because they didn't imagine you pregnant at . . . how old are you?"

"Sixteen."

"They didn't imagine you pregnant at sixteen when you were a little girl but they don't hate you. It's impossible."

Kaylee turns her head, squeezing her eyes shut to keep tears from falling. "Do you have kids?"

"Not yet."

"Then how do you know that?"

"Because I can tell that you're loved. I can tell that your parents have raised you to be a person who helps when someone needs it. A child can't be like that without having first been loved and taught how to help people. Do you know how many teenagers would have helped a crazy woman that they don't even know bring heavy boxes of water into a church?" She laughs, looking at Kaylee. "Very few. So in the few minutes that I have known you, I know that your parents love you and that it's impossible for them to hate you."

Kaylee looks into the cocoa. "My dad got transferred and we were supposed to move in November. Now he's waiting until February, after the baby comes."

Lily waits for more but Kaylee is quiet. She reaches out and squeezes her arm. "Your parents decided to wait so that you weren't moving right when the baby was coming. That's a good thing." Kaylee shakes her head. "It is. They don't want anything to happen to you or the baby and they want to keep you here with your doctor. You don't need to read anything else into that."

"He's starting his job three months later than he was supposed to."

"So what? It's three months out of an entire lifetime. And I'm sure he could move there ahead of you and start working but he's not doing that because he wants to be here." Kaylee looks at her and wants to believe that what she says is true. "Just wait until tomorrow. You'll see it's all going to be okay. It took a lot of tomorrows for my family to be okay but we are."

Kaylee feels a kick under her ribs as if the tiny soul inside agrees. A glimmer of hope flashes through her and for the first time in months the air around her seems different.

"Did you have fun?" Jennifer asks, opening the car door for Avery.

The little girl takes her place in the booster seat and reaches for the seat belt. "I think so. There are some boy angels, they're triplets and they are some really awful kids."

Jen slides behind the wheel and laughs, tossing the script for the Nativity on the passenger seat. "Really? How awful?"

Avery puts two fingers on her face, thinking. "So awful that Miss Miriam's face turned purple." Jen looks at her over her shoulder. "Yeah, it was like her body quit working and she couldn't even talk because they were so terrible."

Jen laughs at the thought but Avery's face is straight, as always. The sameness of her face worries Jen to death sometimes. "I met a girl like me named Sofia, except she has blond hair instead of red."

Jen slaps the back of the seat. "And I met Sofia's dad!" Avery is quiet and doesn't respond, so Jennifer turns forward and starts the car. She's driving past the shops on Main Street, complete with Christmas displays and lights, when she hears Avery whisper something from the backseat.

"I didn't hear you, VV. What'd you say?"

"What color hair does he have?"

Jennifer shakes her head, unsure of what Avery is asking. "What color hair does who have?"

Avery is looking at her mom in the rear-view mirror. "Sofia's dad. Her hair is blond. What color is his?"

This is the first interest that Avery has shown in people in months and Jen smiles, looking over her shoulder. "He has sandy-brown hair."

"Is he tall? Sofia isn't tall."

"He is tall," Jen says, remembering.

"Like Dad."

Jen nods, looking at her. "Yes, like Dad."

Avery turns to look out the window and her eyes appear silver in the streetlights. "So, what's it like being an angel?" She watches Avery in the mirror, willing her to stay engaged, but there is three feet of silence in the car now. Her eye catches the script on the seat next to her and she reads, "Then the angels come." Tears swell beneath her lids at the words. She looks up into the sky and the stars are so thick they look as if they can be stirred with some great wooden paddle. She imagines that sky so long ago as angels spread out against it. The closest of them were surely close enough to reach for and the farthest of them were farther than the most distant galaxy. As shepherds fell to the ground in the angels' brightness, were they baffled by their stillness? Could they literally hear the angels' stillness and feel the beauty and the power at the same time? Jen opens her eyes wider to keep the tears at bay. Were the angels still spread across the sky above her and Avery or were they just beyond this car windshield, within reach? Did they still come with good news? She wipes a tear off her cheek, praying that they do.

Seven

It isn't what we say or think that defines us, but what we do.

— Jane Austen

Gloria stands at the back of the room and smiles, watching Miriam. Her cashmere sweater is pushed up to the elbows, which, according to Miriam, is a no-no for people of quality, and her hair has been shoved behind her ears. For years, Gloria assumed Miriam didn't have ears. With a heavy sigh, Miriam turns back to the Ramsey triplets. "Boys! How can you spread the angelic message of hope and peace amid all this wrestling and talk of flatulence?" It started off as such a charming idea . . . allowing children to be part of the angel choir. All the charm wore off when the nine-year-old Ramsey triplets arrived for the first rehearsal. If Gloria had a dime for every time she heard Miriam tell them to refrain from using the word "fart" or to stop using their sheet music as swords. She had forgotten what little cause nine-year-old boys need to start wrestling on the floor. She and Miriam and a man known simply as Zee have gained several pounds in muscle from extracting the triplets from each other.

"Boys! You are angels!" Miriam says, banging her hands together. She turns to Gloria and shakes her head. "Look what I've done. I've just lied in church." The first rehearsal was a raucous affair, bordering on chaos, but the entire choir soon learned to settle down without being told, so they could see what horrible things the triplets would do next. The boys were proficient at clunking and bonking other kids over the head and possessed uncanny skills at being loud and annoying. For anyone watching, it would seem the boys were headed straight to juvenile detention via the Grandon Community Church Nativity.

James raises his hand at his seat and begins to jump up and down so Miriam will see him. Andrew and Matthew begin to jump as well and Miriam sighs . . . again. The fact that the triplets were named after three of the disciples lost its irony after the first rehearsal. "Yes, Triplet One," Miriam says. She gave up trying to tell them apart during the very first second of that first rehearsal.

"We might not be able to sing in the Nativity."

Miriam's not sure if she should be relieved or exasperated. "What do you mean? Why wouldn't you sing?"

"Our mom might have a baby that night."

Miriam puts a pencil behind her ear. "Your mother may what?"

Andrew raises his hand and Miriam looks at him, holding up two fingers, representing Triplet Number Two. "She's gonna have a baby. We heard her tell Dad she's pregnant again and that it's his fault."

Gloria covers her mouth, smiling, and Miriam nods her head. "Well, if your mother is going to have a baby it is most appropriate for it to be your father's fault. I can also assure you that I just saw your mother and she will not be giving birth on Christmas Eve."

"That's good to know." It's Matthew. Triplet Three. "Because the hospital might get crowded with her having a baby and Jesus being born and all."

Miriam looks at Gloria and the entire choir leans in, listening. "Jesus has already been born and he wasn't born in a hospital," Miriam says. "He was born in a manger.

85

You do know the story, don't you?"

The boys look at one another and James, Triplet One, looks back at Miriam. "What's a manger?"

"Well, it's a place where animals sleep and eat. The hotel was full so Joseph and Mary used the barn for Jesus' birth. They laid him in the feed trough."

The boys' eyes bulge and Triplet Three sticks out his tongue. "Wouldn't the animals try to take a bite of him?"

Now Miriam's eyes bulge out. "Of course not! That's a preposterous notion!"

"Wouldn't they smell him and get him all wet with their big, slimy noses or wouldn't they lick him, since he was lying in their feed trough?"

Miriam has no idea which triplet has said this and waves her arms in the air. "Come now, boys! What does the Nativity *mean*?"

The triplets look at each other and shrug. "It means that if we don't break anything or punch anybody here, our parents will take us out for ice cream," James, or maybe Andrew, says.

Miriam crosses her arms, sighing. "Have you listened to any of your teachers at church for the last few years?"

"We don't go to church. Mom's friend Becky," he says, pointing at a choir member who waves with a sheepish smile, "told her your church needed kid singers so Mom rushed us over here."

"Well, haven't your parents ever told you the story of how Jesus was born? Have they ever read it to you from the Bible?"

The boys shrug. "Maybe," Triplet Two says. "But we've been listening to things for a lot of years now and it's hard to keep track."

The choir members laugh and Miriam claps her hands together. "All right! You'll learn the story as we go along. Let's pay attention to Mrs. Lucien as she plays through each song. Come together now. Let's be sober."

The triplets nod, with as much sober-mindedness as they can muster, but then one of them, the one with the tiny mole to the right of his eyebrow, passes gas and the other two pretend to faint.

"I wonder why their mother ever agreed to allow them to do this?" Gloria asks, as Mrs. Lucien pounds out the introduction to "What Child Is This."

Miriam looks at her, dumbfounded. "Because she needs a break from the army of darkness!"

"Oh, don't be so dramatic," Gloria says. "They're little boys. It's to be expected. Just wait until they have their costumes. They'll be in control."

Miriam watches as they dismantle the room while the remaining children and adults begin to sing. "A straitjacket could not control them."

Don Bunker, owner of Bunker's Hardware, steps to Miriam's side and smiles. "Bunker!" She always feels awkward calling someone by their last name but it's what he insists. "A bright spot of civility. How are you?"

If she had looked harder, Miriam would have seen his chest puff up a little. "Better than I deserve to be, Ms. Miriam." He shuffles and slips a hand into his jeans pocket. "I just wanted to make myself available for any tenor solos during the Nativity."

Miriam inhales and clasps her hands together under her chin. "How wonderful! You are an experienced singer?"

He nods. "I almost sang the jingle for Radiators Plus."

She raises her eyebrows. "Almost?"

"And I've been this close to singing at ribbon cuttings for the Chamber of Commerce."

Miriam smiles, while digging her fingers into Gloria's arm to stop her from trying to sneak away. "And why haven't you?"

Bunker shrugs. "You know how it goes. You rehearse but then they decide to 'go in a different direction' on the morning you practice at the opening of the new carwash." He looks to Gloria and her face turns somber, listening. "That's what they told me. 'We need to go in a different direction.' " He looks at Miriam and waits.

"Yes! Well, we will be assigning parts in the coming days," she says, inching toward the door.

"I also almost sang the jingle for Gray's Pet Store." He begins singing, "If you need a dog, we got that dog. If you need a cat, just like that." Miriam buries her nails deeper into Gloria's arm and backs out the door, waving.

Once they are out of hearing, Miriam gathers herself and puts her hands over her ears. "I can never unhear that. That's how awful it was. It will forever be with me!" Gloria bends over, laughing, as they march into the sanctuary for rehearsal with Mary and Joseph. Miriam gestures for Gloria to sit down and hands her a legal pad and pen. "Take notes, would you?"

Gloria is confused. "Take notes on what?"

Miriam turns to her in a huff. "On the scene, for crying out loud! Every good director takes notes."

"But if you're the director, why am I taking the notes?"

Miriam sighs, balling a fist on her hip. "I am the one blocking out the scene and working with the actors one-on-one. You'll be doing nothing but sitting here. This will give you something to do." Gloria mumbles and takes a seat in the front row of the church.

Audrey Goodrick is a twenty-year-old student at the local cosmetology school. Her reddish-orange hair is highlighted with purple streaks and Miriam pauses, looking at her. "Wasn't your hair brown two days ago?" She is smiling but Gloria fears the strain of it may snap her face in half.

"It was," Audrey says. "But this is the week we start color training. We've been practicing on each other."

"Does the person who did this to you actually like you?" Miriam's smile is strained more than ever.

"Yeah! She's my best friend."

Miriam walks up the steps to get a closer look. "We will need to tuck your hair back into the costume because . . . What is that?" Miriam says, pointing to Audrey's neck. "Is that a tiger's head?"

Audrey smiles, moving the shirt off her

shoulder. "That's my tat! The tiger's crawling up my arm! See the tail down here?" She points to her elbow, revealing the entire length of the tiger.

Gloria wants to burst, watching Miriam's face. Audrey will not be the tranquil, holy-looking Mary of Nativities past, but more like Edna Viviano from the motorcycle shop down the road. Miriam smiles as she pulls Audrey's shirt back onto her shoulder, patting it. "Let's run the lines, shall we? Tom!"

Tom Bradmore is a thirty-year-old auto mechanic at City Auto Service. Miriam "discovered" him while getting her oil changed. Thankfully, he and his family attend the church and have seen the Nativity each Christmas. He was assuming he would simply walk down the aisle, as Joseph has done in Nativities past, to take his place beside Mary inside the stable. But that was the old Nativity . . . not Miriam's Nativity.

"Are you hungry?" Tom asks.

"Hold it!" Miriam says, bounding up the stairs to the platform. "You sound like Tom asking Audrey if she's hungry."

Tom looks at her, reaching for words. "I don't know how else to sound. It's the only voice I have."

Miriam laughs and glances at Gloria who quickly looks down at the legal pad and scribbles "change voice." She then gives Miriam the okay sign and Miriam nods. "You see, you need to picture the scene in your mind. Joseph and Mary have been traveling for miles and miles. She's been up on the donkey and Joseph has been trudging along, beside her." Miriam demonstrates walking as if Tom is unfamiliar with the practice. "So, now you're taking a little break from your travel. Mary is off the donkey and the two of you are leaning against a hillside." She looks over her shoulder to Gloria. "We will have a representation of a hillside, correct?"

"No, we won't."

Miriam shakes her head, as if something is shooting out the top of her brain. "What do you mean we won't have a hillside?"

Gloria writes "no hillside" on the legal pad. "This isn't Broadway, Miriam. It's Grandon. I could get you a few ficus trees, if those would help."

Miriam's mouth is gaping open and closed as if she's trying to ingest a word in front of her. "Really, Gloria? Ficus trees in Israel?"

"It was just an idea," Gloria says, writing on the pad.

"It was a terrible idea."

Gloria makes the sound of a canary in shock and says, "Miriam, there are no terrible ideas when people are brainstorming."

"There are terrible ideas *and* terrible people. You brought both to the table." Gloria's pen is set afire as she writes. "Would you stop writing down everything I say?" Gloria raises her arms in surrender and looks at Tom, winking. "What can we have here? Could we have something that looks like a rock?"

Gloria purses her lips and looks up at the ceiling, as if the rocks can be seen there. "That's probably doable."

Miriam rolls her eyes and turns back to Tom. "So, you will help Mary lean against a rock because she needs a break and then you say your line." She runs off the platform to the seat next to Gloria.

Tom takes a big breath. "Are you hungry?"

Miriam springs to her feet. "That's good! That's good! But make it sound a little less like you're asking the guys watching Sunday afternoon football and more like you're asking a pregnant woman, who's been on the back of a donkey for three long days."

Tom shakes his head, confused. "I'm pretty sure I'd say it the same way."

Miriam's mouth thins into a straight line and she sits down, looking at Audrey. "Okay! You lean against the rock and Joseph asks if you're hungry and you say?"

"Yeah. It won't be long before he comes."

Miriam leaps to her feet again and Gloria covers her mouth to keep from laughing. "The line is actually *yes*. Not yeah. It's the first century and 'yeah' wasn't invented yet."

"Yeah," Audrey says. "I get that but these lines don't sound anything like I'd say. I'd say, 'Yeah, I'm starved.' "

Tom steps forward, holding his script. "And I wouldn't say, 'We need to continue on.' I've never said anything like that. When I'm trying to get my wife and kids in the car I just yell, 'Come on! Move it!' "

Miriam flinches as he yells and bounds up the steps once again. "You would say 'Yeah, I'm starved' or 'Move it' because we live in the twenty-first century. They talked the way they did because they lived in the first century."

Audrey and Tom are baffled.

Miriam presses her hands together and touches her fingertips to her chin. Her mouth has petrified into a confused scowl. "Every period movie that has ever been made has been written in the dialogue of that time period. That's what makes them believable."

"I don't think I've ever seen one. Aren't those always boring?" Audrey asks.

"Those are girl movies, right?" Tom says.

For once in her life, Miriam is speechless. Her face is blank.

Gloria stands and moves toward the stairs, looking at Audrey. "It's like trying to use a scroll in an iPad world or an iPad in a scroll world." She looks at Tom. "Or trying to use a spear in a Ruger world."

Audrey's face lights up and Tom nods. "Right!" Audrey says. "Scrolls would be lame."

"No hunter worth his salt would head out with a spear."

Gloria smiles, nodding. "Right! It doesn't work because it's out of place." Her salt-and-pepper curls bounce around her face and she turns, grinning at Miriam and hands her the legal pad. "Could you write that down for me?"

"It's not that I don't like my job," Gabrielle says. "I do! I just think I'm in the market for something more stimulating. Does that make sense?"

Jennifer reaches for the mass of chicken wire and tries to form it into the shape of a rock. She wants to be kind and understanding but is annoyed by this conversation. In the last three years she has discovered that most people have a great fondness for talking about themselves. She and Gabrielle have worked together for three days and she knows where Gabrielle went to college, where her brothers live, and her favorite movie. Gabrielle, on the other hand, knows everything there is to know about Ryan and nothing about Jennifer. The more she talks, the more Jennifer finds her voice like clattering metal pans.

"Makes sense to me," Ryan says.

Gabrielle smiles and Jen catches Ryan smiling back. She feels foolish for getting her hopes up. Gabrielle's face is always shining, her clothes freshly laundered, modern, and cute. Jen's face often looks tired and her clothes are always three to five years behind modern and rarely have that freshly laundered look. She's not opposed to wearing something two days in a row. Jen feels that Gabrielle is the fresh catch of the day and she's like the day-old bread that sits on the counter of Betty's Bakery — still good but just not as fresh.

"We have to go back and eat at Maggio's again. That was fun," Gabrielle says.

Ryan and Ed hoist a wall into place. "It was great," Ryan says.

"I'll have to take you to Perk's, too," Gabrielle says. "It's a hip coffee shop. They don't have all the homemade stuff like Betty's but it's a younger crowd. I go there a lot and just read after a stressful day or listen to the live music. You'll love it!"

Jen smiles but has the sickening sensation of being back in high school. Gabrielle has done nothing to her but she finds herself envying Gabrielle's "stressful day" kind of life and the ordinariness of just sitting down and reading a book. She's angry about having crushlike feelings for Ryan, a man she barely knows, and feels she's somehow dishonoring Michael.

She is ready to go home at the end of Avery's rehearsal but Avery is hungry. "How about a bowl of cereal when we get home?" Jen says.

"Can I get soup to go from Betty's?" Jen begins to shake her head. "Please, Mom? We haven't gotten soup there in so long!"

It's on the way home and the line is short so maybe it won't take long. Jen looks around the bakery-restaurant and sees lots of older faces and families with kids. It looks like Gabrielle is right. All the young, hip adults must be at Perk's. This had been a favorite spot of hers and Michael's. She looks behind her at the corner booth where they sat just eight years ago, two years before Avery entered their lives.

"That new coffee shop has opened across town," Jen said to him. "It's called Perk's."

"I know," Michael said. "I was driving by last week and stopped in." He was wearing a black sweatshirt and a ball cap was pulled down over his mass of brown waves.

"Was it good?"

"Yeah, it's real vibey. Live music. Lots of young college guys. I felt like an old dude among all those hip cats. If you ever get tired of me you can have your pick at Perk's!"

Jennifer laughed. "Have your pick at Perk's! An awesome slogan." She reached over the table and grabbed his hand. "But what if I like the old guys at Betty's? I'd take a good-old-fashioned-burger-and-piece-of-apple-caramel-pie guy any day over a decaf-pumpkin-latte guy."

Michael grabbed hold of his stomach. "Well, if it's a burger body you want, you've come to the right place."

She leaned toward him. "And if anything happened to me, would you come here to find a raspberry-cream-cheese-pastry girl?"

He shook his head. "Oh, no! I'd be over at Perk's checking out their skinny soy-Frappuccino girls." She smacked his hand but couldn't help laughing.

"How fun seeing you here!"

Jen turns and forces her face to smile at Gabrielle and Ryan, in line behind them.

"Would you like to eat with us?" Ryan asks.

She feels Avery looking up at her. "Thanks, but we were just grabbing some soup to go."

"And a chocolate chip scone," Avery says. "Dad's favorite."

Jen sighs. "And a chocolate chip scone," she says, too tired to argue.

"Is this your daughter?" Gabrielle asks. "She's so cute! I see your eyes but the rest of her must look like her dad."

Jen looks at Avery and smiles. "She does look like her dad."

She's grateful that it's her turn to order, and when she and Avery move to the end of the counter to wait for their soup, she looks for something hidden and unreachable at the bottom of her purse. She pretends not to see Gabrielle and Ryan sit at the booth together where she and Michael sat years ago and convinces herself she can't hear Gabrielle's steady laugh or smell her perfume, wafting throughout the restaurant.

She reaches for Avery's hand. "Let's go home, VV. I'm tired."

"She's pretty. Don't you think, Mom?"

Jen reaches for the white bag on the counter filled with their order. "Yes. Gabrielle's very pretty." She means it. The last three and a half years have taught her that she's never more in touch with life than when so much of it hurts.

EIGHT

God asks no man whether he will accept life. This is not the choice. You must take it. The only question is how.
— HENRY WARD BEECHER

Lily and her husband, Stephen, sit in a booth at Betty's Bakery. Large plastic ornaments hang from the ceiling and a decorated Christmas tree sits in the corner of the restaurant. The windows have all been etched with fake snow, with electric candles glowing on each sill. Stephen opens a manila folder, looking over the paperwork one final time. The two met in college where Lily was attracted to his sense of purpose and quiet character, not unlike her dad's. It didn't hurt that he loved bicycling and hiking. His hair is just as thick and dark as it was in college but his goatee is flecked with gray. Lily thinks it makes him look distinguished for his work at the bank. For the first four years of their marriage, Lily and Stephen lived in Louisiana, where he worked in sales and Lily for a nonprofit. Although they enjoyed the work, the heat and humidity was, in Lily's words, devastating. That and the distance from each of their families compelled them to find work closer.

"Lily?"

Lily turns and smiles at Kaylee. "Hey, Kaylee!" she says, getting up and hugging her. "This is my husband, Stephen."

Stephen stands and reaches his hand out for Kaylee. "Kaylee from the other night, right? Nice to meet you. Lily told me all about you. Meeting you ended up being the highlight of her week." Kaylee smiles and tucks strands of hair behind her ear. "I don't know what you talked about but she came home in a great mood, so feel free to talk with her anytime because I like it when she comes home that way."

"You say that as if I always come home in a bad mood!"

"Those are your words, not mine," Stephen says.

Lily laughs and rolls her eyes. "Are you here for lunch?" she says, looking at Kaylee.

"I'm meeting my mom here. She's getting off work at lunchtime so we can go to an appointment."

Stephen indicates the side of the booth next to Lily. "Feel free to sit with us while you wait," he says, gathering the paperwork and sliding it back into the folder. "Would you like a pastry? I can get one for you."

"No, you don't! You are not going to use Kaylee to get yourself a pastry," Lily says.

"That was not my intention," Stephen says. "Honest."

Lily laughs. "Honest! Right! We just had a huge conversation about food choices," she says, looking at Kaylee. "I said that just because we're at Betty's, doesn't mean we *have* to eat a pastry."

Stephen slaps his hand on the table. "And I said, why didn't we just go to the grain and sprout restaurant for the meeting?"

Lily laughs harder, pointing her finger in the air. "Number one, there isn't a grain and sprout restaurant. Number two, I didn't choose the meeting place. Dorothy did."

Stephen growls, leaning his head in his hands. "So what can I order? A big bowl of grass? Maybe a handful of berries and twigs?"

Lily shakes her head. "He has it so rough. I'd like to keep him around for a few years, so I encourage healthy eating. But what do I get from him?"

"Anything you want!" Stephen blurts out.

Lily leans onto the table, laughing, and Kaylee smiles listening to them. "For ten years I've been listening to her about how to eat, and the day I want a pastry with my lunch, she says no."

"You had two doughnuts for breakfast!"

Stephen shoots her a look that says she's crazy. "What does breakfast have to do with lunch?" He raises both hands and swipes them in the air. "That's all I'm saying."

"Do you always argue like this about food?" Kaylee asks, confused. Stephen's laugh is like an exploding note from a trombone, making Kaylee laugh, too. She felt it the first time she was with Lily and feels it again sitting here with her and her husband, that feeling of being okay. She often imagines what adults think, when they look at her pregnant belly. They remember their own sophomore years, filled with basketball, football, cheerleading, choir, and sleepovers, and can't begin to imagine what the sophomore year of a pregnant teenager looks like. Does she still go to sleepovers or meet her friends at the mall? Does she hear students whisper about her as she walks through the halls and does she have anyone to sit with at lunch? They never ask these things but Kaylee imagines the thoughts playing out in their minds. Lily and Stephen don't look at her in those ways.

"I'm sorry," Stephen says. "Your parents are probably normal people and we have completely freaked you out."

Kaylee shakes her head. "Oh, no! They're not normal, they're just like you guys." She hadn't meant it to be funny but it came out that way and the three of them laugh, together. Her eyes widen and she places her hand on top of her belly. "Wow! The baby is going crazy right now."

"Can I feel it?" Lily asks, her face open with surprise. "It's been years since my sister was pregnant and I haven't felt a moving baby in a long time and would love to." Kaylee reaches for Lily's hand and guides it to the spot just above the navel. Lily smiles. "Wow! This is one active baby!"

A grin spreads across Stephen's face. "A future running back!"

"It's always about football with him," Lily says. She bends toward Kaylee's belly and says, "Hello, little one. Merry Christmas! You're going to make the perfect gift."

Stephen watches Kaylee's face. "What would you like for Christmas?"

"I haven't really thought about it."

He looks at her over his coffee mug. "You haven't thought about it? When I was a kid

I started dropping hints about Christmas in June."

"You still do that!" Lily says.

"Of course I do! It's a big deal!" He sets the cup down with a thud to make his point. "So what's on your list?"

"It's been kind of a weird Christmas, in case you didn't notice," Kaylee says, trying to smile.

"But the weird situations are where Christmas really shines," Lily says.

"So what do you want?" he asks. "And you can't say stuff for the baby."

Kaylee thinks, playing with the zipper on her coat. "Some money for clothes that fit would be great, and a new cell phone cover."

"That's it?" Stephen says. "I doubt that will be any problem for Santa."

"Santa hasn't stopped by my house in a few years," Kaylee says.

"Well, we'll write a letter ourselves and clear that up," Lily says. "I'm sure he's just had too many pastries and he's suffering with brain fog."

Steven groans. "Even Santa isn't exempt from your food rants."

"The last time I saw him here at Betty's he had two pastries on his plate!" Lily says.

"And I don't think Mrs. Claus helps any," Kaylee says. "She's overweight, too, so you know the entire year she's making lots of pies and cakes and covering everything he eats with cheese sauce."

Stephen's face falls. "And I thought you were my friend." He lifts his hand when he sees a woman in a maroon woolen peacoat approaching their table. "Dorothy, you have saved both me and Santa!"

Kaylee takes her cue and scoots to the end of the booth, getting up. "I'll see you later," she says, looking at Lily.

"I hope you can bring your parents to the Nativity. We'll be doing it twice on Christmas Eve. I'd love to see you again before the baby comes." She stands and hugs her tight, whispering, "Remember, everything will be okay." She holds Kaylee's shoulders and looks at her. "Everything."

Somehow, when Lily says things will be okay it's not some pie-in-the-sky hope but rather the audacious hope of Christmas that Kaylee feels. She nods. "I'll tell my parents about it. Nice to meet you," she says to Stephen. Then leans to whisper, "I'd let my husband get a pastry."

Stephen punches his fist into the air. "And she swings back around to my side!"

As if she's been sold out, Lily moans, "Oh, come on!"

Kaylee walks to the other side of the

restaurant and sits at a table where Lily and Stephen can't see her but, when she cranes her neck around a post, she can see them and the woman who has taken her place at the booth. Kaylee watches Lily and Stephen, and while moments earlier they were laughing with her, their faces are now serious as they pore over the papers in the folder. She has never been to see a Nativity program at a church before and can't imagine wanting to go, but for whatever reason, she feels the nudge that Lily talked about to see one now.

They are asked to wait in the reception area and Kaylee's mom, Joni, picks up a magazine as she stares up at the TV. The volume is down but it is a cooking show, complete with tiny bowls filled with spices and a mound of beef that is being manhandled and roped into submission.

"I've never used strings when I've cooked a roast," her mother says. Kaylee isn't paying attention. "I wonder if tying it up like that somehow makes it more tender?" She looks at Kaylee. "I always just throw it in the crockpot but maybe I'm missing out on that string method. What do you think?" Kaylee lifts her shoulders, studying her phone. "Maybe on the way home I should buy a roast and some string, huh?"

"I don't care, Mom."

Her mother turns her attention back to the TV. "Well, we have to eat. It won't hurt to try this."

"Then try it."

Her mom sighs, twisting her wedding band. "I'm just nervous, Kaylee."

"Why should you be nervous?"

"Why should I be nervous?" Her worn expression and slumped posture gives away her exhaustion. "This decision, this child changes all of our lives for the *rest* of our lives. It's not just you. It has never been just you. From the moment you got pregnant it's been about all of us. So yes, I'm nervous."

Kaylee is quiet. She hears the sadness in her mom's voice and knows she's right but she doesn't want to say that. She doesn't want to say anything or even be here. They watch the cooking show in silence. "I never meant to get pregnant, Mom." It is the closest thing to an apology Kaylee can offer today.

Her mother takes hold of her hand. "I know that. I can't imagine any sixteen-year-old setting out to get pregnant." She squeezes Kaylee's fingers. Her mouth turns up in a sad, small smile. "I'm so sorry,

Kaylee."

Kaylee is ashen-faced. For months, she has been angry at her parents, at Jared, her friends, at the school and the idiot kids inside it, but mostly at herself. In her times of deepest anger, she has hated her parents more than Jared but never knew why. They have been the ones to stay by her side, to rearrange their schedules, to take her to appointments, and now to apologize for something that isn't their fault.

Kaylee looks up at the television. "Things always look easier on TV."

"That's because writers resolve things in thirty minutes or an hour."

Kaylee studies her phone. "How would they resolve this?"

Her mom is quiet. "It doesn't matter. What's on TV isn't real. Even the real stuff is rarely real. It's edited."

"No editing here," Kaylee says to her phone.

They both watch as the cook on TV rubs a blend of seasoning onto a roast and then ties it together.

"You know, everything *does* look easier on TV. I'd either pull the string too tight and the roast wouldn't cook well or I'd leave it too loose and the roast wouldn't cook well."

Kaylee stares up at the screen. "I want you to stick to your regular crockpot roast. There's been enough changes at our house for now." Joni laughs and leans over, bumping her shoulder into Kaylee's.

When Kaylee's name is called it is twenty-five minutes past the appointment time. They are led down a short hallway and into a small office with a cluttered desk. The woman behind the desk smiles in recognition. "Well, hello there."

"Whoa," Kaylee says, sitting down.

NINE

Gratitude is the heart's memory.
— FRENCH PROVERB

Gloria called two days earlier wondering if Jen could swing by her home to sew some of the angel costumes. "I'll be at practice with Miriam but I'll leave you a key so you can come in. I'll have pie," Gloria told her.

"I'd do it without the pie," Jennifer had said, but looks forward to the treat she rarely has time to make herself.

She watches Avery's face in the rearview mirror and knows her thoughts are flapping around as if on a mast, her hands twisting in the act of remembering. Jen feels a pang of heartache and a rush of sadness but mostly pride as she looks at Avery. All that is precious to her in this world comes down to the fifty pounds in the backseat.

The house is warm, with the scent of pinecones, as Jennifer opens the door. She

112

has been in Gloria's home only once, for a Glory's Place present-wrapping party a few Christmases ago, before Gloria married Marshall. Now, pictures of the two of them together sit on side tables and line the entry walls, along with photos of their blended family of children and grandchildren. "She said there are some toys over there in the corner," Jen says, pointing into the living room. Avery finds them and reaches for a Barbie in a long purple dress and a pale plastic horse with a mustard-colored mane, as her mother goes upstairs.

Jen walks to the end of the hall, where a third bedroom has been converted to a sewing room. The sewing machine sits in front of the window. A pile of thick, rust-colored fabric sits at the side of it, in line for creation. An ironing board stands against one wall, draped with pieces of flowing gold and silver fabric. A small hanging rack, lined with coat hangers, holds the rest. These are the pieces that are to be sewed into costumes for the angel choir. Her phone rings inside her purse and Jennifer digs for it. "Hello."

"Mrs. De Luca, this is Marianne with Dr. Plantiga's office. I got your message regarding your husband."

Jennifer sits on the chair in front of the

sewing machine and feels something swelling inside her throat. "Yes, thank you for calling me back."

"Is this about insurance claims?" Marianne asks.

"No. Nothing like that. I was just hoping that I could speak with Dr. Plantiga. I'm trying to contact all of the medical personnel who helped my husband."

The line is quiet on the other end. "Mrs. De Luca, I don't mean to sound insensitive but I don't understand. If this isn't about insurance claims then what —"

Jennifer interrupts her. "I'd like to thank everyone who helped Michael."

She hears Marianne sigh on the other end of the phone and imagines her smiling. "I understand. I'm sorry for my confusion." Jen's eyes fill at the sound of her tone. "It's just that a call like this is so rare."

"It's my fault. I wasn't clear in my message. For the longest time, I've been looking for answers, but in the last few weeks I've realized I may never have any answers but maybe I'll be able to close the gap a little by thanking everyone who did everything they could for Michael." A tear falls down her cheek and onto her hand and she brushes it away on her jeans. Marianne sets an appointment and Jen hangs up the phone, dry-ing her face.

The angel costumes are finished and hanging now in Gloria's sewing room as Jen cuts two pieces of chocolate chess pie for her and Avery. They jump as the kitchen door opens. "Oh, hi," Ryan says, letting Sofia enter before him. He looks at Jennifer and tries to keep from smiling. After an overnight stay in Riverside and a long day of house hunting there, the day has suddenly brightened and the air has become warm and full.

"I didn't know you were going to be here," Sofia says, taking off a rainbow-colored scarf.

Avery talks with her mouth full. "I didn't know you lived here until I got here. I played with your toys."

Sofia grabs Avery's arm. "Come on! Let's go play some more."

Avery looks at her mom. "Um," Jen says. "We should get going."

"Ahh," Sofia says. "You just put the pie on your plate. Can we play till you finish eating it?"

Avery's eyes are huge as she waits for Jen's answer. "Okay," she says. "For a few minutes."

Avery shoves a big bite of pie into her

mouth, before setting down the plate and running into the living room with Sofia.

Jennifer leans against the counter and looks at Ryan. "I'm sorry. Miss Glory wanted me to sew some of the costumes. She said the house would be empty and that she'd leave pie for us." She laughs at the thought. "I never would have cut this if I'd known you . . ."

Ryan takes off his coat and hangs it over the back of a chair at the kitchen table. "If she left the pie for you then you better eat some. She will take it as a great offense if you don't. Surely, you know how my aunt feels about food."

She looks at the pie. "Would you like a piece? It's delicious."

He walks to the sink and washes his hands. "I'm sure it is. I think I've gained five pounds in my time here." He reaches for a fork out of the drawer and takes the pie from her, leaning against the counter.

"Ed and I finished the rocks today for the set," she says. "They look great. The whole set looks really good."

He smiles. "I never knew that I'd add rock making to my skill list."

"Are you any closer to deciding on the job you want to take?"

He takes a bite of pie and bobs his head

around, thinking. "Maybe. We saw a house today the color of pink yogurt and Sofia said it didn't matter what it looked like on the inside because she wanted to live there. Period." Jen laughs, thinking about it. "Thankfully, the inside was awful so we could take the Yoplait house off the list." He points with his fork toward the living room. "Sofia really wants to live here."

"And how about you? Where do you want to live and work?"

He looks at her and smiles but turns his eyes to the pie. "I want to live where Sofia is happy. It doesn't matter. Ground-floor apartment, duplex, condo next to a play-ground. I can live anywhere." He takes a bite and uses his fork to cut off another piece, looking at it. "We found a house the second day we were here that she loves, but that one already has a contract on it. Plus, if I had moved on that one, it would mean that I had decided to take the Hazelton job. And I don't think that's how I'm leaning."

Jen thinks for a moment. "Really? River-side is sounding better?"

He nods. "I think. I don't know. It's tough. Both jobs would be great. We did find a house in Riverside that's right in my price range. I actually think I'm going to put an offer in tomorrow. I'll sleep on it and call the Realtor to talk it through again."

She feels disappointed but smiles anyway. "I'm sure Miss Glory was hoping you would be closer. Some others were probably hoping you would be closer, too." She looks at him. "Gabrielle is a sweet woman."

Ryan picks at his pie, moving it around on his plate. "She is." He looks up at her. "I'm sure I'll be bringing Sofia to Grandon a few times a year so Aunt Gloria can load her up with pies and cookies."

"You're a good dad."

He smirks, taking a bite. "Be sure to tell Sofia that when I'm asking her for the umpteenth time to make her bed or brush her teeth or put her dinner dishes in the dishwasher."

"Or take a bath," Jennifer says, relating. "Or pick up her toys or put her dirty clothes in the laundry basket or close the bag inside the cereal box."

They laugh together and Ryan moves to the kitchen table. Jen notices how he moves away. He glances at her and smiles, not a warm smile but a distant, life-is-complicated kind of smile. "Will Sofia see her mom at Christmas?"

"No. We take turns at the holidays."

"That must be tough."

"It's not great but it works. Sofia likes

Julie's husband so that makes it easier."

Jen stays at the counter, picking at her pie to make it last. "What's Julie like?"

He looks at the table, pushing his empty plate away. "She's like Sofia."

That's all he says and she watches his face. "Well, Sofia's wonderful, so —"

"Sofia is, yes," he says, cutting her off. It's obvious he doesn't want to talk about Julie. "What about your husband? What's his name?"

"Michael."

"What does Michael do? How did he manage to not get roped into helping with the Nativity?"

"Mom?" Jen looks up to see Avery standing in the doorway. She gives her mom a wary eye and takes the empty plate from her, setting it on the counter. "It's time to go."

"Don't you want to finish your pie?" Jen asks.

Avery grabs her hand. "No. We need to go now. We need to eat dinner. I want you to cook Dad's favorite." Jen opens the dishwasher and begins to place her plate inside. "Come on, Mom!"

"Stop it!" Jennifer whispers, looking into Avery's eyes. "We are not going to be rude."

Avery's eyes fill with tears. "Its time to go home."

"Are you leaving already?" Sofia asks. "We just started to play."

Jen walks to the entry and reaches for her and Avery's coats out of the closet. "Maybe you could come over to our house sometime, Sofia. Would you girls like that?" Sofia nods as Avery pushes her mother from behind. Jennifer ignores her and looks at Ryan. "Could you let Miss Glory know that the sewing is finished and her pie was delicious?" He smiles and closes the door, watching as they get into the car.

Jen sits in silence behind the wheel, looking down at her hands. "That was very rude, Avery."

The voice is small and unsure in the backseat. "We need to go home."

"I'm allowed to talk to men."

"You shouldn't be."

Jen turns to look at her in the stillness of the car. "Yes I should. It's okay."

"It's not okay. It's all wrong."

"No it's not, Avery." She feels herself getting flushed and takes a breath. "We have to talk to people. We have to be kind."

"No we don't."

"Yes we do!" She lowers her voice, sighing. "Sofia and her dad were only being nice to us. That's all. We respond to them in kindness, not by being rude."

"I don't like him."

"You're not allowed to say that because you don't even know him."

Avery's face twists up in confusion. "Do you know him?"

"No, not really. I've worked with him on the set. That's all." She reaches over the seat and squeezes Avery's leg. "I know you're sad and hurt and confused and angry but that doesn't mean you can hurt other people."

Avery is quiet, staring out the window. "You like him, don't you?"

Jen's face gets soft. "He's a nice man."

"But do you like him?"

"He's a nice person."

"You think he's handsome, don't you?"

"He's not bad to look at."

Avery turns to look at her. "Do you like him more than Dad?"

She shakes her head. "No. I love your dad."

"Then you shouldn't be talking to other men." Her face is angelic and rebellious and Jen smiles, too tired to tackle more of this on a mostly empty stomach.

"Let's go home."

Avery looks out the window. "That's what I said."

Ryan watches as Jen starts the car and pulls away.

TEN

What is to give light must endure burning.
— VIKTOR FRANKL

Jennifer runs down the hallway and flips on the bathroom light before opening Avery's door. She is wailing in her bed as Jen sits down next to her and grabs her by the shoulders. "Avery! It's okay! It's okay, VV. Mommy's right here." The sheets below her are wet and Jen slides off the bed, kneeling beside it to stroke Avery's face. "Avery! Avery!"

Her eyes are wide and she wraps her tiny arms around Jen's neck. She begins to cry and holds on tighter.

"It's okay. You're with me."

"You were gone. You were gone and I was alone!"

Jen pulls her head back, so she can look at Avery in the half-light. "It was just a bad dream. Everything's okay now."

Avery looks at her through swollen eyes and realizes what she has done. She pulls her legs close to her. "I did it again. I'm sorry, Mom." She begins to cry and Jen sits up on the bed next to her.

"These are just sheets. They're easy to wash. It's no big deal."

Avery rests her head on her mom and wraps her arms around her. "You were gone. It was real."

Jen kisses the top of her head and squeezes her. "It might have felt real but it wasn't. I'm not going anywhere. It was just a dream."

"How do you know you're not going anywhere? You can't know that."

Jen looks out the window and hopes for the right thing to say. "You're right. I can't know that. But Dad and I would never willingly leave you. Nobody could even drag me away from you because I'd be strong like Superman."

"Come on, Mom! Superman?"

Jen smiles, squeezing her. "Spider-Man?"

"Not even close."

Jennifer's gasp fills the room and she laughs. "Who, then, if not Superman or Spider-Man?"

Avery thinks for a moment. "Dora the Explorer!"

The quiet explodes with laughter and Jen squeezes Avery. "Well, Dora is always resourceful and bright and has some awesome friends who help her along the way, so I'll take it!" She thinks for a moment. "Not even Wonder Woman?"

Avery shakes her head. "She's so fast. I've seen you run."

Jen rubs her forehead. "So I have the superhero capabilities of a six-year-old cartoon character?"

Avery nods. "It's how it is, Mom."

Jen groans. "Let's keep this between us, okay?" They sit for a moment and she asks, "Was Dad in the dream?"

"For a second but then he went away again."

Avery had whispered it, so Jen had to strain to hear. She rests her cheek on the top of Avery's head and wonders if Avery will dread sleep because her dreams will be filled with Michael for the rest of her life or if one day she'll look forward to them.

"Is he happy, Mom?"

Jennifer makes a noise in the back of her throat as if she's thinking. "Much happier than us."

"How do you know?"

Jen turns her head to see out the window. "There's no sadness in heaven. He wouldn't want us to be sad, either, but that's impossible for us here, isn't it?"

Avery nods. It's the most she has spoken about her father in over a year, since Jen started taking her to see Dr. Becke. Jennifer waits for more but Avery is finished for the night. "Come on," she says, sliding her legs off the bed and opening the top drawer of the dresser. "Let's get you into something dry and into my bed."

"What about my sheets?"

"They can wait until morning."

Avery stands and begins to walk toward the door, when she turns around and pulls the blankets up over the wet spot. Jennifer watches and her heart breaks. Since Michael died, Avery has been covering up aches that can't bear the light of day. Jen reaches for her hand and they walk through the hall together.

"We are doomed!" Miriam says, putting her head on the table.

Gloria sets a cup of coffee in front of her and pokes Miriam in the shoulder. "Sit up before Ryan and Sofia come in here and think you're having some sort of conniption."

Miriam ignores her. "The angel choir is filled with beasts, Joseph and Mary are hardly in this century, let alone in the first, and the shepherds are always talking about ways to take out the sheep."

"They're from the hunting club! What were you expecting?" She takes a bite of pie and chases it with some coffee.

"Which triplet did we make the Angel of the Lord?"

Gloria thinks. "Andrew, I think. No, I'm positive it's Andrew. Nearly positive. It could be Matthew. Or even James."

Miriam rubs her head. "Did you hear him last night as he repeatedly said, 'Listen to me! *The* baby of all babies has been born'?" She looks at Gloria. "*The* baby of all babies has been born!" She throws her hands in the air. "How many times did I tell him that the line is, 'Unto us a child is born. Unto us a Savior is given'?"

Gloria laughs, thinking about it. "But he was so cute with his little finger pointing in the air. And you know what? Every time he said it a chill ran down my spine. 'Listen to me! You don't want to miss this! *The* baby of all babies has been born! No other baby, before or after, will be like him'." She reaches over and pats Miriam's hand. "It feels this way before every Nativity. Everything will pull together."

Miriam leans onto the table, looking at

her as if she has just been awakened after a week-long sleep. "Will it really?"

"Of course. Eat your pie."

Miriam looks at her plate. "Who eats pie at nine-thirty in the morning?"

Gloria takes a bite and makes yummy noises in her throat. "Respectable people with great taste, that's who."

Miriam takes a bite and cocks her head as if to say it's not such a bad idea after all. "So, you're saying that all the varied discussions of farts and boogers among the angel choir will somehow pay off in the end?"

Gloria raises her eyebrows and sticks her fork in the air. "Sure! That's what I'm saying!"

"Aunt Gloria, do you have a thermometer?" Ryan is walking through the living room, toward the kitchen.

"It's up in the bathroom. What's wrong?"

"Sofia was complaining that her stomach hurt her yesterday but it was after dinner and she had had two pieces of pie so I assumed it was because she ate too much. She's complaining again this morning and when I touch her it feels like she has a fever."

Gloria leads him upstairs and retrieves the thermometer from the bathroom closet. She follows Ryan to Sofia's bedroom, where the little girl is curled up on the bed. "You don't feel well, babe?" she asks, feeling her forehead and sticking the thermometer in her ear. Sofia shakes her head. "Do you hurt anywhere?"

"Down here," Sofia says, rubbing the bottom of her stomach.

Ryan sits on the bed next to her and touches her head. "She still feels hot."

Gloria removes the thermometer and reads it. "One hundred point eight." She looks at Sofia. "Does your stomach hurt like there's a pain in it or does it feel weird, like you're going to throw up?"

"It's a bad pain."

Gloria glances at Ryan. "Have you thrown up or had diarrhea?"

Sofia keeps her hand on her belly, moaning. "I had diarrhea this morning."

"You didn't tell me that," Ryan says. "How many times have you gone?"

"Two. And it feels like I have to go again."

Ryan looks at Gloria and she nods. "Okay, I'm going to take you to the emergency room." He is pulling the blankets off Sofia and helping her sit on the edge of the bed.

"Can I go in my jammies?"

"Go comfortable," Gloria says, reaching for Sofia's slippers on the floor. "That's my motto." She slips the shoes onto Sofia's feet and squeezes them, smiling at her.

As Sofia stands, she bends over in pain, moaning.

"I got ya," Ryan says, scooping her up and walking down the stairs.

"Open the door, Miriam!" Gloria says.

Miriam jumps up from the table. "What's happened?" she asks, stepping into the living room and reaching for the door.

"Sofia's sick," Gloria says, running after Ryan. "I'll pick Marshall up at the store and we'll be right behind you," Gloria says, reaching for Ryan's coat and following them to the car.

"You don't have to come, Aunt Gloria," Ryan says, helping Sofia into the car. "I can call you."

Gloria shakes her head. "You might need something while you're there and either Marshall or I can do all that running around for you." She leans into the car and kisses Sofia's face. "I'll be right there, sweet lamb." She and Miriam stand in the driveway and wave as Ryan pulls away.

Jennifer opens the pantry door and grabs a handful of potatoes, setting them in the sink to wash. She clicks on the TV in the living room and finds the five o'clock news so she can watch it as she prepares dinner. The potatoes are diced, along with carrots, onions, and celery as stories about a robbery in the city and what's happening in the state legislature fills the screen. She is sautéing the carrots, celery, and onions when news of a car accident on the highway seizes her attention. A female reporter is on the scene as police lights flash behind her. "It appears the SUV crossed the median into this line of traffic," she says, indicating the highway. "Again, three people have been taken to University Hospital and are in critical condition at this time." Jen watches the screen as the vegetables sizzle on the stove.

She was laughing. It was December and she and Avery had gone to visit friends in Garrett. It was dark when she began the twenty-mile drive back into Grandon. For some reason, Avery giggled in her car seat. She had giggled so few times since Michael died in June, that Jen turned to look at her. She didn't see the SUV cross the median. She's grateful for that. Time tumbled, careened, and crawled in the next few moments.

It was so dark she could barely make out the approaching shape but could hear the words that came as if through thick webs. "Oh, God! Help them!" Its clothes were dark, black-dark with a tall hat. *Scrape-rick, scrape-rick* was the noise it made. It whimpered like a child. Or was that Avery? She had to get to Avery. She tried to turn her head to see her but she couldn't. The voice disappeared, perhaps the tall hat was flat on its belly in the muck. She moved to try to help it but there was no face. She couldn't see a face or even the shape anymore. Sirens were wailing somewhere or was that a shout or a cry? Was it her own cry she was hearing or Avery's? She felt something on her shoulder and wanted to reach for it, thinking it was Avery. "Can you hear me?" the voice at her shoulder said. It was the tall hat. "It's freezing. Where's your coat? God, help these people." She felt something warm around her neck. "This will help a little."

The siren was distant. The tall hat was somewhere behind her and said, "Here you go, sweetheart. Look, sweetie! This is for you. Help this little girl. She's afraid. Shh, shh, shh." The siren was closer and more frantic. "Here you go, sweetie. This doll's for you." The noise stopped. "Your daughter is okay," Tall Hat said, touching Jen's shoulder. The web grew thicker and voices sounded displaced, while shapes moved and floated, lifting her out of that cottony dream. She had a broken collarbone and three broken ribs but Avery came away from the accident without a scratch.

Jen smells the vegetables and rushes to turn off the burner. She reaches for the phone, dialing. "Hi, this is Jennifer De Luca and I have been trying to find out the names of the paramedics who were first on the scene of an accident I was in with my daughter three years ago. I've made a couple of other calls in recent weeks but I've never heard from anyone."

"I'm so sorry to hear that, Mrs. De Luca," a woman on the other end says. "Have you checked over your own medical records from the accident?"

Jen dumps the diced potatoes into the pot and adds a container of chicken stock. "I have but there's no indication of who the paramedics were."

"Do you remember who you left a message for?"

Jen adds some salt and pepper to the pot. "Monica."

"Let me find her for you."

Please, not another voice mail, Jen thinks, adding parsley and stirring.

"Mrs. De Luca, it's Monica. I'm so sorry I didn't get back to you before now. You had said that the paramedics were the first responders that night?"

Jennifer leans against the kitchen counter,

remembering. "Yes."

She hears computer keys clicking in the background. "According to hospital files, paramedics arrived shortly after the local fire and rescue unit."

"That was the tall hat . . ." Jen says, her voice fading.

"I'm sorry?"

"I remember a tall hat. I didn't realize that fire and rescue was there as well. Thank you so much."

She hangs up the phone and turns to click off the TV and sees Avery, who has been listening.

"Who were you talking to?"

Jen sits at the kitchen table and reaches for Avery's hands. "A woman at the hospital, who is trying to help me find everyone who helped us the night of our accident."

Avery's face closes and her mouth draws in. Her eyes are dark with what looks like fear. "Why are you doing that?"

"Because I think it could help."

Avery is shaking her head as tears fill her eyes. "No, no, no, no, no!" She yanks her hands from her mom and tries to get away.

Jen stands and reaches for her arm, turning Avery so she can see her face. "One of those people who helped us actually cared enough to say a prayer and give you the angel doll. I remember it and want to say thank you. I think it will help me."

Avery's face is red and puckered. "It won't. You keep bringing up all this bad stuff but it never helps."

Jen pulls her toward the table and lifts her onto her lap, as she sits. "I don't keep bringing it up. It's just here. All the time. And so many things remind me of that night and of your dad. I need to do something to help myself and I think that by thanking all of those people, I'll get one step closer."

"You won't." Her little face is defiant, unbelieving.

Jen rests her head on top of Avery's. "I might." She says it almost like a prayer and breathes easier for the first time in ages.

ELEVEN

Hope is being able to see that there is light despite all of the darkness.

— DESMOND TUTU

"You brought her in before the appendix burst so we'll be able to go in and remove it." The doctor looks at Sofia lying on the exam table, tapping her on the leg. "And that means you'll be feeling better very soon."

Dr. Hernandez is kind, with small lines feathering out at the edge of his eyes and flecks of gray high-lighting his thick shock of brown hair.

"What is an appendix?" Sofia asks.

"It's a finger-shaped pouch that sticks out from your colon right down here," he says, touching her lower belly on the right side.

"But if you take it, what will happen to me?"

He smiles and leans against the table.

"Nothing." He shrugs. "You won't even miss it, and do you know why?" She shakes her head. "Because we're not totally sure what it does." Her eyes are big. "It's true. It has to have a function, right?" She nods. "But after years and years of medicine no one really knows what it is! Some believe it helps our immune system. We do know that sometimes it can get blocked and cause lots of pain. It can also leak and rupture, but your dad got you here before that happened." He smiles and is moving toward the door, indicating he's ready to proceed.

"How long does it take?" Ryan asks, holding Sofia's hand.

"Not very long. Laparoscopic surgery is just a few small incisions, which means less scarring and shorter recovery. She'll spend a night, maybe two before going home, but downtime isn't very long." He smiles at Sofia. "Someone will be in shortly."

Ryan leans down and kisses her forehead. "You're going to feel so much better in a little while."

"I don't want to do this. It's scary."

He sits on the table and squeezes her leg. "You'll be sleeping through all of it. This is something that Dr. Hernandez does every day and he said himself that it doesn't take very long. Plus, you'll really be able to milk this with Aunt Gloria and get all of your favorite foods."

"You mean like ice cream and cookies?"

He nods. "If I know her she'll probably sneak them into the hospital."

She stares up at the ceiling, thinking about it and smiles. "Do you think she would make me a chocolate chess pie?"

He winks and nods, whispering, "Consider it done."

"Will you call Mom?"

He pulls his phone out of his jeans pocket and dials Julie's number, handing the phone to Sofia. During the last three years, he has had his share of hard feelings and names for Julie, but now he feels sorry for her because she's not here to hold Sofia's hand or kiss her face when she wakes up from surgery. He wishes she were here for Sofia and realizes it's the first time he's thought that since the divorce. He listens as Sofia relays the events of the last eighteen hours. He knows Julie will have lots of concerns about the surgery and questions for him, and for once, he doesn't dread the conversation. Maybe he's growing up or maybe it's one of those Christmas miracles his aunt Gloria talks so much about.

Jen waits just inside the choir room as the

angel choir finishes "Do You Hear What I Hear?" and smiles, watching Avery sing, her mouth forming a perfect red O. She is so serious, taking the responsibility of spreading the good news squarely on her shoulders alone. As the final note is sung, she makes a beeline for Jennifer. "Mom, Sofia was in the hospital."

"What?" With the set nearly complete, the set team had the night off, so she didn't see Ryan.

Avery is putting on her coat. "Her 'pendix was broken so they took it out yesterday."

Jen looks around the room for Gloria or Miriam. "Her appendix?" She spots Miriam and Gloria and leads Avery to the other side of the choir room.

Miriam looks tattered and disheveled, as if someone has just taken her down from a shelf and blown the dust off her. She bends down to pick up scattered song sheets. "Ramsey boys! Remember to practice the songs before you give me my first gray hairs!" she says, yelling over her shoulder at the triplets. "And Andr—" She stops, not attempting any of their names. "Angel of the Lord, what is your line?"

He pauses and then smiles, thrusting his finger into the air. " 'Listen to me! *the* baby of all babies has been born!' "

Miriam's mouth is open, about to correct him . . . again, but she shakes her head, smiling. "That's right! '*The* baby of all babies has been born!' "

"And you said that king . . ." It's Triplet One, bending nearly in two to scratch the back of his leg. "He had it in for Jesus and tried to get rid of him?"

Gloria nods. "King Herod *tried* to get rid of him but his plan failed."

"Somebody should've told him he couldn't be king anymore," Triplet Three says. "They should have punched him or kicked him or run him over with their bikes."

Gloria shakes her head. "Well, we don't punch or kick or run people over with our bikes."

The triplets pull on their coats. "You're sure the bad king didn't win?"

"Positive," Miriam says. "In the end the good king wins."

"The king of all kings, right?" Triplet Two says, socking one of his brothers in the head just because he was standing there.

"That's right!" Gloria says.

"This is what I would've done to him," Triplet One says, punching Triplet Three in the stomach. Triplet Three bends over, pretending to be in pain and grabs Triplet

Two around the waist, knocking him to the floor.

"Oh, for the love of . . ." Miriam says, waving her arms. "Take it into the hallway!" She turns, spotting Jen and Avery, and pretends to pull out her hair.

"Sofia is sick?" Jen asks.

"Poor lamb," Gloria says. "She was so sick. They operated yesterday morning and took her appendix out. She got home this afternoon."

"She's okay?" Jen asks.

"A bit of pain," Miriam says. "You know how it is following surgery. But now that the problem is gone, she will be on the mend."

"How's Ryan?" She feels Avery watching her.

"Very well. Making her laugh. And Gloria made her a chocolate chess pie, which the child cannot even eat yet, so it feels more like torture to me. Or maybe it's that Gloria feels like torture to me. Sometimes I just don't know."

Avery tugs on Jen's coat sleeve. "We have to go see her, Mom."

"I'm not sure if we'd be allowed to do —"

Gloria holds the loose music sheets together and taps them on top of the piano. "She would be over-the-moon excited to see you, Miss Avery!"

They haven't crossed the room before Avery says, "We need to go home first. I need to get something for Sofia."

Once they're home, Jen waits at the edge of the sofa as Avery runs to her room. "Okay, I'm ready," she says, running back down the hall. The angel doll is tucked under her arm. "Let's go."

"Is that what you're giving her?"

Avery is hurrying to the door. "Yeah. Come on."

"Wait!" Jennifer walks to her and touches the doll. "But you love this doll. You've had it since the acci—" She stops. "Why would you want to give it away?"

"Mom, let's go!" It's the only thing she says and she stands, looking at her mother.

Nodding, Jen turns Avery to the door and closes it behind them.

Ryan opens the door and smiles.

"Is this a good time?" Jen says.

He stands aside. "Sure! Come on in."

Jen feels that odd catch in her chest again as she moves past Ryan to the couch where Sofia is propped up watching *America's Funniest Home Videos*. An empty cup of Jell-O sits on the coffee table. "We're so sorry you were sick. Are you feeling better now?"

"Bleh," Sofia says, giving her a thumbs-down.

Jen rubs Sofia's arm. "Did it go well?" she says, looking at Ryan.

He's wearing camouflage pants with a black T-shirt and black zip-up sweatshirt. His gaze settles on her and she twists the wedding band on her finger before crossing her arms. "It went very well. She was in and out in no time and the doctor doesn't expect a long recovery. Hopefully, she'll be feeling better tomorrow."

Avery sits on the end of the sofa and holds out the angel doll. "I brought this for you."

Sofia reaches for it. "Cool! She's so pretty! Thanks!"

Ryan turns his head, looking at the doll. "Huh." He sticks his hand out. "Can I see her for a second?" He makes a low, rumbling sound in the back of his throat and shakes his head.

"What are you looking at, Dad?" Sofia says, taking the doll from him.

"Nothing. It just reminds me of a doll your mom and I gave you a few years ago."

Sofia plays with the angel's wings, spreading them with her fingers. "No you didn't."

"I'm pretty sure we did."

She rolls her eyes, looking at Jen and Avery. "Dad, I remember every toy you and

Mom ever gave me. Trust me, you never gave me an angel."

He shrugs, smiling at Avery. "Maybe that's because only angels can give angels."

"We would have come earlier if we'd known you were in the hospital," Jen says. She watches Avery and Sofia play with the doll and whispers to Ryan, "I'm sorry about the other day. Leaving so abruptly."

He waves a hand in the air. "No apologies. I get cranky, too, when it's dinnertime." He avoids looking at her too long. The longer he stands close to her and the more time he spends working next to her, building the set, he realizes he always feels some sort of wintry calm around her that he shouldn't feel.

A roar like a waterfall pounds inside Jennifer's head. She wants to talk, to sit down over coffee and ask him such familiar questions as *Where did you grow up? How did you become a contractor? Who is Sofia most like? What's your favorite food?* And such unusual questions as *What's a great day look like for you? How about a bad one? What would you do differently in your life?* Jen thinks of Gabrielle and Avery and smiles. Things are still too complicated, too hard.

"How are rehearsals for the angel choir going?" Ryan asks.

Avery shrugs and shakes her head. "Eh. We're not very good. We sing 'Joy to the World' and trust me . . . it is not!" Ryan falls onto a chair, laughing, and Avery's eyes widen. "I'm serious! It's awful!" His laugh is deep-rooted and pops like gunfire when it lets go.

"She's right!" Sofia says. "We stink."

Ryan laughs again and Jen joins him. Avery and Sofia look at one another and roll their eyes, causing Ryan and Jen to laugh harder. They laugh because they are tired and because they are grateful and because, for a few seconds, their girls lift a bit of the world off their minds.

TWELVE

I will love the light for it shows me the way, yet I will endure the darkness because it shows me the stars.

— OG MANDINO

Kaylee opens a drawer and pulls out a stack of T-shirts, packing them into a box, before opening the sweater drawer and doing the same. She reaches for the wooden jewelry box she painted and decorated when she was in third grade, on top of the chest of drawers. She's careful as she lays it on top of the sweaters. The clay pig from kindergarten makes her smile because the legs are way too short and the tail is much too long. She wraps it inside a T-shirt and places it next to the jewelry box. Pictures from softball and tae kwon do are also wrapped in newspaper, along with snapshots of friends and family trips to Yellowstone, the Grand Canyon, and the Statue of Liberty.

In a few minutes, she moves to the closet and begins to fold pants, shirts, and jackets, placing them inside the boxes, and then shoes, boots, belts, and bags. The emptying space swallows her. Her face begins to quake, her eyes getting wet and glassy, but she pulls it back together, good as new, when she hears her mother in the hallway.

"Are you packing?" Joni asks, sticking her head inside the bedroom door.

"A little." Kaylee steps out of the closet, carrying a box. "I didn't want to wait much longer and be as big as the moon doing this." She sets the box on the floor at the end of her bed and looks around. "I hate moving."

Her mom sits on the bed. Her brown hair is held back by a headband and she looks tired. "I do, too. There's so much to do."

Kaylee sits next to her. "No, I mean I hate *moving.*" She sighs and her mom puts her hand on her leg, patting it. "I thought I'd love leaving but I'm going to miss this room and this house and this awful town that I couldn't wait to get out of."

She can't see her mom's face but Kaylee knows by the shaking in her voice that the end of her nose is red. "This is where we brought you home from the hospital on the day you were born. We laid you in the crib right over there, and when Adam came along, you insisted that we put the crib right there again so you could watch over him at night. You even told us that you would get up and feed him in the middle of the night. That never happened, by the way."

Kaylee laughs. "It was a great house to grow up in. A great town. I can't believe I think that."

"I won't tell anyone." Her mom glances at Kaylee's artwork that she has hung on the walls and the door of her room since kindergarten and wipes her eyes with her sleeve. "I've lost track of all the last times with you and Adam because they are coming at me so fast now. You know, the last time I had to tie your shoes for you. The last Little League game I went to or the last batch of cookies I had to make for a Valentine's party. This will be the last time I'll see all of these pictures that you have colored or painted over the years. It's like closing a museum."

Kaylee smiles, looking at the drawing of her mom with the stick legs and long spaghetti-like hair and the rocket ship painted pink with purple hearts. "I'm scared, Mom."

Her mom kisses the top of her head. "I won't lie. It is scary."

"I've done a lot of dumb things."

"So have I. And don't even get me started on your dad!" Kaylee laughs as she wipes her nose with her palm. "There are lots of decisions when you're a parent. Sometimes you get them right. Sometimes you get them wrong."

"I don't want to start off getting them wrong." Joni rubs her hand over Kaylee's back and Kaylee remembers her doing that every night, at bedtime. Her parents told her this day would come, that she'd grow up and move on. It felt like the day would never get here but now that it's this close, it feels like her throat is slipping down to her stomach. So this is growing up and moving on and looking forward and leaving behind. It would be hard enough on her own but the life kicking inside of her reminds her that there are two of them now. Her child will never know this house or walk with her through the historic square and picture-book gazebo. Her child will never shop with her for toys at Wilson's department store like she and Adam did with their mom or share a pastry fresh out of the oven at Betty's Bakery. Life was moving on for both of them.

Jennifer works at applying another coat of joint compound to one of the rocks the team has made from chicken wire and strips of canvas, while Gabrielle helps Ryan secure more two-by-fours into a rock, on which Mary and Joseph will be able to sit. Ed and two others are busy spreading joint compound over the stable walls, making them look like the inside of a cave.

They are busy, there is still much to do before Christmas Eve. Gabrielle sings along to "Baby, It's Cold Outside" and coaxes Ryan to join her. Jen keeps her head bent to her work and listens. She and Michael would sing this song together and end up in a heap of laughter. They were so bad. She still remembers all of it like it was yesterday. At first the memories would sweep over her in great waves of grief. As time has moved on, she's come to realize that when she remembers Michael, it means that she carries who he was with her. He left a mark that can never be erased. A smell, a landmark, a song, or even a burger can summon him back to her mind. And in those moments, she can still see his face and hear his voice. She prays again that Avery will come to realize that as long as she remembers her dad, he'll never be truly gone, that when she's sad, her dad's memory is comfort, and when she feels ecstatic, he's part of why she feels that way. If Avery tucks him away from her thoughts, Jen is convinced that a huge part of who she is will be lost.

"Did you hear that, Jen?" Jen turns to Gabrielle and realizes she hasn't been listening. "Did you hear that Ryan is taking the job in Riverside?"

Jen reaches for the bucket of joint compound. "Yes. I heard there was that possibility."

"I thought you liked both jobs equally," Gabrielle says, hiding her disappointment well, Jennifer thinks. "Why didn't you settle in Grandon?"

Ryan glances at her and Jen before turning back to his work. "I don't know. It was just going to be difficult to live here."

"I hope there's something that will bring you here to visit," Gabrielle says. Jen would love to think that Gabrielle is being coy or even desperate but she's not. She's a kind person who is genuinely going to miss another person.

"Of course I'll be back!"

"You must be talking about my nephew defecting." Gloria is standing by the door and shaking her head. "Breaks my heart."

"Riverside's only four hours away," Ryan says.

"Too far," Gloria says. "The older I get, the more I become jealous and greedy and want family closer." She surveys their work and claps her hands together. "Miriam will be tickled pink to see that Mary will be able to sit down on a rock. I knew my brilliant nephew would think of something." She looks at Jen. "Isn't he great, Jen?"

"He is," Jen says. She feels embarrassed after she says it and looks at her watch, realizing she and Avery will be late to see Dr. Becke if she doesn't leave. "I'm sorry, I have to take Avery to an appointment." She grabs her purse and coat and hugs Gloria on the way out.

Gloria steps to Ryan as he reaches for another two-by-four. "Jen is so sweet," she says, whispering to him. "Don't you love working with her?"

"Actually, no. No, I don't." He moves to the sawhorse and misses the look on Gloria's face.

"How are rehearsals going?" Dr. Becke asks. She looks at her notes. "You are part of the angel choir, correct?"

Avery nods, holding Homer on the sofa. "We're not very good yet."

Jen smiles and Dr. Becke laughs, leaning down and propping her elbows up on her knees. "Do you mean you don't know the songs yet?"

Avery shakes her head. "No, I mean we stink. The boy angels always fight, especially the triplets. They are always in trouble and nobody can sing while they're fighting."

"It sounds like the angel choir needs a therapist!"

"I don't think you could help."

Dr. Becke leans back and claps her hands, laughing, and Jennifer shakes her head. She hadn't expected that from Avery. Dr. Becke reaches over and puts her hand on Homer's head, squeezing it. "Listen, I wanted you to come in a couple of days earlier than our scheduled appointment because I was looking at the beautiful picture you made of the balloon for me." She gets up and pulls out the pushpin that holds the picture to the board above her desk. "You know, even though I've been through lots of schooling and have been in practice for over twenty-five years and even have the word 'doctor' before my name, you have taught me something, Avery." The little girl's eyes are wide. "Since you colored this balloon for me, every time I sit at my desk I get to look at it. A couple of days ago, I was on the phone and looking at this beautiful picture again, when it came to me."

"What?" Avery asks.

"Well, since you are unable to call your

dad, I thought that you could write a letter to him, and when you're done, you, your mom, and I will tie it to some helium balloons and release it."

Avery is still, thinking. She bounces Homer on her knees and then looks at Dr. Becke. "What do I say in the letter?"

"Everything you have wanted to say to him every time you have reached for the phone. Good or bad." Dr. Becke looks at Jen and she nods as a small smile forms.

"I don't want him to think that I'm mad at him because he left. I don't think I should say that."

"Say whatever you feel," Jen says. "If it were me, I'd want you to tell me."

Dr. Becke walks to her desk and opens a drawer, pulling several colors of paper from it. "I bought all sorts of stationery so you could find just the right one." She holds them in front of her. "Here is one with the Disney princesses, this one is pink with sparkly stars on it, this one has a border of red hearts around it, butterflies are the theme of this one, and then there's just all sorts of colors, some with sparkles, some with animals as the background, and some that just have words like 'love' and 'hope' written on them." She sets the stationery down in front of Avery and moves back to her desk, retrieving a plastic box filled with pencils, pens, crayons, and markers. "You can write the letter here today during our time or you can take it home, if you're not sure what you want to say."

Avery sets Homer on the sofa and leans over, picking up the stationery. "I know exactly what I want to say." She riffles through the pages and selects a light blue piece with sparkly hearts and stars. "Will you and Mom read it?"

"Only if you want us to."

"I just want Dad to read it." She reaches for a red pencil. "I only know how to spell a few words. We get new spelling words every week."

Dr. Becke smiles, sitting on a chair and resting her arms on her knees. "That's okay. Just spell what you can," she says, looking at Jen.

The letter takes close to an hour as Avery sounds out each word in her head, before writing it. Avery keeps her head down and concentrates on every letter. When she finishes, she reaches for another sheet of paper, green this time, and draws a heart that takes up most of the page. She colors a quarter of an inch or so in red and then another quarter inch in yellow, aqua, purple, green, and so on until the heart is a rainbow of color. She writes, "I love you Dad, Form Avery" across the top and holds it up for her mom to see.

"I don't know what his favorite color is anymore. So I used all of them."

Jen smiles and feels her heart quivering. "He'll love it."

Dr. Becke walks to her desk for an over-sized envelope and hands it to Avery. "When you finish, just put the letter and the picture in here and we'll take it outside."

Avery holds the letter in front of her as if she's proofing a document about to be sent to the printer and then carefully folds it and the heart, before inserting them into the envelope and sealing it.

Dr. Becke holds out her hand. "All set?" Avery nods and Dr. Becke opens the door to her bathroom. Avery peers around her and sees a few colorful balloons, bobbing against the ceiling. She grins and reaches for the long strings, gathering them together. Dr. Becke uses a hole punch to create two holes on each end of the envelope and then loops the strings through them, tying them together in a knot and securing the letter. "Does it feel ready for flight?" Avery touches the string and the letter and nods. "Ready to launch it?" Avery holds the balloons and leads them through the reception area and outside to the parking lot, where the air slaps at their cheeks, turning them red. "You pick the spot," Dr. Becke says.

Avery looks around and chooses the side of the building, where there is a patch of grass struggling to breathe beneath gray, mournful-looking snow. Her breath comes out in small clouds as she looks into the sky. Dr. Becke catches Jennifer's eye as Avery releases the balloons. They stretch their necks, watching as they climb. It's as if the balloons catch strength from the air and are called higher and higher, until they are out of sight.

THIRTEEN

Everything has its wonders, even darkness and silence . . .

— HELEN KELLER

"That's exactly what Ryan said: 'No, I don't,' " Gloria says, baffled. "Who wouldn't enjoy working with Jen De Luca? She's so sweet."

Miriam is pacing in the choir room. "Maybe they had some sort of argument."

"About what? Which nail to use?"

"It doesn't matter!" Miriam's waving her arms over her head. "I have a genuine crisis here and you are stewing over a comment that you probably didn't even hear correctly."

"I heard it fine. I just don't understand why he said it."

"I don't understand why you are so nosy," Miriam says beneath her breath and sifting through the sheet music.

Gloria snaps her fingers, pointing. "I heard that, too! And I am not nosy. I'm just concerned."

Miriam slaps the music down on the piano top with a huff. "About what? Why are you slighted that Ryan doesn't enjoy working with Jennifer?" Gloria shrugs and Miriam's eyes light up. "Oh, I see! You had Jen work on the set because you wanted her to think that your nephew was cute."

"I did no such thing." Gloria's hands are on her hips.

"I think thou dost protest too much. And you do not look at all convincing wearing a sweatshirt with Snoopy in a Santa hat." Gloria opens her mouth and Miriam talks over her. "You're like some odd Christmas cupid who reeks of mulled cider and cake. You thought you could put two people in a room together and that love would blossom, but now you are distraught because your sad plan has failed. Your nephew is not interested."

Gloria sighs, sitting on one of the chairs in defeat. "How could this happen? Ryan is twenty gallons of delicious."

"That just sounds so wrong on every level, coming from his aunt."

Gloria puts her hand in the air to stop Miriam. "And Jen is kind and smart and so pretty and a wonderful mother."

Miriam sits next to her and slaps Gloria's thigh. "The sooner you discover that people are the absolute worst at setting other people up, the better off you'll be."

"Lenny was a wonderful match for you!"

"First off, his name is Lenny. Second of all, he took me to the Chuck Wagon for their early bird buffet. I've never choked down a sirloin at four o'clock in the afternoon before. Last, he had me home by six because he had to watch *Jeopardy* with his mother." Gloria hangs her head. "Can we move on to my crisis?" Gloria nods. "Ed has to go out of town on business and his flight does not get back in town until the evening of the twenty-fourth, so he can no longer sing the solo in 'Go Tell It on the Mountain.' We don't have any other tenors."

"Well, we have —"

"No we don't!" Miriam snaps, unable to hear what Gloria has to say.

"He's the only experienced tenor in —"

"Almost singing the jingle for Radiators Plus is not experience, Gloria!"

"Let me put it another way . . . all of the other men have said that they do not want a solo. Bunker is the only one who wants to sing a solo. He asks us every time he sees us. He asked in the Christmas card that he sent me and Marshall, and he asked Marshall if he could sing for him at the store and made a mess of 'The Little Drummer Boy,' right there in the middle of the shoe department." Miriam shakes her head. She can't even comprehend it. "The Psalms tells us to make a joyful noise." Miriam stands. "Where are you going?"

Miriam looks at her. "To call the noisemaker."

After an hour of driving, Jen and Avery pull into the drive for the town of Garrett's Fire and Rescue Department. The building looks like a three-car garage. She parks away from the big garage doors and she and Avery walk to the entrance. "Thank you for coming," Jen says, looking at Avery.

"You made me."

Jen smiles. "I didn't make you. I asked you."

Avery shrugs and looks at the door. "Let's just go do it and get it done." She takes her mother's hand and they walk through the door.

A simple metal desk sits in the middle of a mostly bare room. A long, black vinyl sofa sits in front of the window with a matching armchair against a wall. Various pictures of fire and rescue squad members line the white walls. Two yellow trucks with GAR-RETT FIRE AND RESCUE written on the sides can be seen in the spacious garage to the left. "Hey there! Hello," a man says, walking toward them from one of the trucks. He is for all intents and purposes bald, save for a few sprouts of hair, and wearing mustard-colored pants and a white T-shirt with the fire and rescue circle logo on the left breast. "Can I help you?"

Jen extends her hand, smiling, as she puts her other hand on Avery's shoulder, drawing her close. "My name is Jennifer De Luca."

"Rick."

"I live in Grandon, and three years ago we were in a car accident on the highway, and from what I understand, this squad was the first on the scene."

Rick nods, pointing to the sofa. "Please. Sit down." He sits in the chair and rests his forearms on his knees, listening.

Jen likes him. He somehow puts her at ease and she wonders if he's the one who gave Avery the angel. "I was wondering if there's any way to find out which of your squad members helped us that evening." He looks concerned and she holds up her hand. "Nothing is wrong. You see, someone, one of the men from the squad, was actually praying for us that night. He even put a scarf around my neck and gave my daughter a doll. We just want to find him and say thank you."

Rick rubs his head with both hands. "Wow, that —"

"I had a feeling it might be too hard," Jen says.

"No, that's not what I was going to say. We're able to keep pretty accurate files these days. It just doesn't sound like one of us." Jen's face falls as he adds, "I don't mean to say that someone here wouldn't pray or give a girl a doll, but there's always so much communication going on between the squad members, and things are moving so quickly, that it seems unlikely that any of us could slow down long enough to do those things." Her eyes tell him that she has come here placing all of her hope inside this building, and he rises to his feet. "But let's get on the computer and find out who was there that night." He moves to the desk and sits down. "What was the date?"

Jen walks behind him and looks at the computer as Avery stays on the sofa. "December 3, 2011."

He clicks open one file and then another before mumbling to himself and opening another application. "Ron knows his way around this computer better than any of us but he's not here today. Hold on." He leans onto the desk, getting closer to the screen. Several clicks later, he makes an "aha" sound. "Two vehicles. A 2006 white SUV and 2003 black Nissan on the northbound lane of —"

"That's it," Jen says, reading over his shoulder.

"Lane Reinholdt was there. She's been part of the squad for about ten years now."

"It wasn't a woman," Jen says.

"And it looks like Randy Mayhew was there."

Jen looks at him. "Randy Mayhew? That's him, I'm sure. Is Mr. Mayhew here today?"

"He's probably at work. We're all mostly volunteer."

Jen glances at Avery. "Does he work nearby? Could I go talk to him?"

Rick doesn't say what's on his mind, that there's no way on earth that Randy prays for himself, let alone anybody else, but rather stands and digs into his pocket, pulling out his keys. "Let me tell the others I'm stepping out and you can follow me. Randy works over at the co-op."

Randy's on the loading dock when they pull into the parking lot, throwing large bags of grain or seed or cement mix, for all Jen knows, into the back of a pickup truck. He is young, maybe in his mid to late twenties, with a blond crew cut and stout legs. "Rick! My man! What's up?" Randy watches as Jennifer walks toward him and looks at Avery, staring at him from the back of the car.

"Randy, you and Lane were first responders three years ago when this woman was in a car accident."

He jumps down from the loading dock, forming a triangle with Rick and Jen.

"You gave my daughter a doll," Jen says, her breath rising like steam in front of her. His face is blank and Jen talks faster, hoping to jog his memory. "An angel doll. My daughter was in the backseat and I was driving. You prayed for us that night and put a scarf around my neck."

"I . . ." Randy looks to Rick and his face is solemn, not knowing what to say.

"I came here to thank you," Jen says, her voice sounding urgent. "It meant —"

"It wasn't me," Randy says, not letting her finish. He looks again at Rick. "I'm sorry, ma'am, but I've never bought a doll in my life or had one with me when I've been on duty." Rick looks at the ground, hoping to find something that will help there.

"But it had to be you. The hospital said you were the first on the scene. You had on a black coat and some sort of high black hat and you gave me your scarf."

Randy shakes his head, apologetic. "Our coats are yellow."

"Could have been another motorist," Rick says. She looks at him. "Our squad might have been first responders but that doesn't mean we were first on the scene."

Jen is quiet, searching their faces. "Of course." She smiles at Randy, moving to wrap her arms around him. "Thank you." She pulls back and looks at him. "Thank you for everything you did for us that night." Randy puts his hands into his coat pockets and shuffles his feet. She hugs Rick and says, "Thank you, Rick. Thank all of you for what you do." The men are embarrassed and Jen moves to her car. "And thank you for helping me today." She gets behind the wheel and drives through the parking lot.

"I told you it wouldn't help," Avery says, keeping her voice low.

Jen's throat is full as she keeps her eyes on the road. "But it did help."

Ray Elhart stands on the side of the tractor as his seventeen-year-old grandson, Micah, drives it toward a group of evergreens. "Those there," Ray says over the sound of the engine. "Those are small enough that we can ball and bag them." Some customers liked to replant the tree after Christmas so they need to dig up the root ball. "Since there's only six days until Christmas, let's just dig five and we'll need to cut at least another fifteen for the lot." Ray and Micah move to the wagon behind the tractor and reach for shovels, the chain saw, burlap sacks, and rope. As he lifts the sacks from the wagon, something catches Ray's attention in a group of trees to his left.

"How about this one, Grandpa?"

Ray is distracted, walking to the trees.

"Grandpa?"

He turns to see Micah standing by a tree, ready to dig. "That one's great!" Ray pulls the knit cap farther down on his head as he reaches for a wad of deflated balloons, tangled among the branches of one of his evergreens. He pulls the mess of strings and flimsy balloons from the tree and begins to twist and smash them together, when he notices an envelope. He turns it over to the front: "For Daddy." He opens the envelope and pulls out a blue piece of stationery, a letter written in a child's handwriting.

Der Daddy

ive mist you so muc sins you went uway

Mommy sez you ar in hevin and you cant come back but sez you ar happy up ther. I trid to col you but you cant her the fon. i wus mad at you for leving but Mommy sez you wud hav stad if you cud

I wont you to no I miss you evre day and I love you ol the tim.

Mommy kriz a lot when she fenks i cant see becoz she missus you to. you ar a grat dad and I hav yor piktur by my bed when you and me ar lafing on my brthday.

I am in frst grad and me and Mommy hav a crismis tree. I hop an angl givs you this and a hug and a kiss.

i love you i love you i love you

Avery

Ray opens a separate green piece of paper with a colorful heart on it that says, "I love you Dad, Form Avery."

"Grandpa! Are you coming?"

Ray waves at his grandson and walks toward him, reading through the letter again.

"What gives, Gramps?" Micah asks, digging around the base of a tree.

"How good are you on the computer?"

Micah stops his work and looks at his grandpa. "Pretty good. Why?"

"Think you could find an obituary without having the name of the deceased or the date he died or even the place where he died?"

"What?"

Ray hands the letter to Micah. "This little girl's dad died. All we have is her name." Micah studies the letter and glances up. "Could you find something?"

Micah hands the letter back to Ray. "Maybe."

Fourteen

Sometimes our light goes out but is blown into flame by another human being. Each of us owes deepest thanks to those who have rekindled this light.

— Albert Schweitzer

Sofia runs through the empty house, heading for what will be her bedroom. "This is it! This is the one I want." She looks out the window and begins to unlock it. "Look, Dad! I can just crawl right out my window and be in the backyard."

Ryan laughs. "You're not a thief. You can use the door, like normal people."

Susan, a graceful and graying Realtor who has made a career of selling homes, stands in the doorway, smiling.

Sofia darts through the hallway. "I love the triangle-shaped closet under the stairs. It's the perfect size for me."

"Which means, I'll never be able to store

anything in there because it will be filled with tiny chairs and tea sets and stuffed animals," Ryan says.

Sofia grabs Ryan's hand and swings it back and forth. "Don't worry, Dad. One day I'll be too tall and won't be able to play in there anymore. But right now I can, and boy, am I going to have fun! Big-time!"

Ryan and Susan laugh as Susan glances at the calendar on her phone. "How does the twenty-second look to sign papers?"

Ryan looks at Sofia and smiles. "Looks like a great day to buy a house!"

Jennifer, Gloria, Miriam, and Lily pass out a costume to each angel choir member and ease it over the heads of the children. The Ramsey triplets begin flapping their arms like wings. "No, no!" Miriam yells. "You are not birds."

"We know that! We're pterodactyls," Triplet One says.

Triplet Two begins to caw like that prehistoric bird and flaps around Triplet Three. Triplet Two climbs onto a chair and jumps off, flapping his wings as the other two climb atop chairs of their own. Miriam bangs her hands together again. She has had enough. "Andrew, Matthew, and James!" Everyone stops and stares. Miriam has seldom used the triplets' names. "You are not pterodactyls, bats, eagles, or any bird of prey. Once and for all, you are angels."

Triplet One, his blond hair standing on top of his head like a yellow wad of cotton candy, stops and says, "I thought angels protected us like our own police."

All eyes are on Miriam. "Yes, that is true. Angels protect us."

"Then how can they protect us, how can they fight the bad guys, if they're just standing still like you want us to?"

Gloria steps behind Miriam, whispering. "He's got a point."

"Oh, shut up, Gloria!" Miriam hisses.

"Angels are big," Triplet Three says, raising his arms above his head and standing on his tiptoes. "They can beat the crap out of bad guys."

Miriam pats the air in front of her. "Yes, yes, of course they can beat the crap out . . ." She catches herself and sighs. "Angels are mighty and fierce and majestic and they are also messengers. When they announced that Jesus had been born, they weren't fighting or jumping off chairs! They were excited because they were spreading the good news." She is waving her arms and dancing across the choir room floor. The triplets are in awe, their eyes bugging out as they watch her. "They had been waiting for this day, and when Jesus was born, they couldn't wait to fill the sky. Think about the light! Think about the radiance! Think about those shepherds, looking up at the most beautiful sight they'd ever seen." Miriam stands still, looking up at the ceiling and then drops to her knees. "How can you see something that beautiful and stay on your feet? You can't. It's impossible. That's how beautiful those angels were!" She scrambles back to her feet. "That's what everyone who comes through the front door of this church should feel when you come singing down the aisle. They should feel the beauty. They should feel their hearts swell three sizes bigger because you are announcing the greatest news on earth." She stands, looking at the Ramsey triplets, and their little faces beam with something like understanding — or gas, it's hard to tell with them.

Gloria begins to clap and the entire angel choir breaks into applause. "If only you'd thought of that three weeks ago," Gloria says.

"It's only been three weeks?" Miriam says, shaking her head.

Jennifer and Lily pass out battery-operated candles to each child and adult.

"No real candles?" Triplet One bellows.

"For so many obvious reasons," Miriam says, winking at him. "Remember," she says above the noise. "Children walk in first, followed by adults, and be sure you sing out because many of you will still be in the lobby as we enter singing. All right, line up and let's head to the sanctuary for our final practice!"

She hears Bunker practicing his solo for "Go Tell It on the Mountain" and he sounds like an out-of-tune tire iron tumbling down a metal slide. He struggles to find the notes and sticks his finger inside an ear, to better hear himself. His voice rallies round to gathering many of the right notes and he looks at Miriam, thrusting his thumb into the air. Oddly, Miriam feels an excitement replacing the dread that has clung to her for so many days, and she rushes ahead of the choir, waving like she's directing planes.

"And she's back," Gloria says, ushering the children down the hall.

Lily feels her phone vibrating and lifts it out of her back jeans pocket, just before it goes to voice mail. "Hello!" she says, sticking out her arm to indicate a straight line for the children.

"Lily! It's Dorothy. Is this a good time?"

"Uh." Lily covers her other ear. "We're about to go into dress rehearsal for the

Nativity."

"We can talk later but I wanted to see if you and Stephen would be up for a Christmas baby."

Lily stops, the line of choir members moving past her. "What did you say?" She can hear Dorothy chuckle.

"We have a mom who's about to give birth any time now. She's chosen you and Stephen if you want the baby."

Lily's eyes spill over and she leans against the wall. "What? It took months last time and then . . ." The mother changed her mind, leaving Lily and Stephen with a roomful of baby things but an empty crib. "When? When is she due?" She can sense Dorothy smiling.

"Technically, she was due yesterday so it could be any minute, really."

Lily is flapping her hand. "I have to call Stephen. Does she want to meet us? Will we know when she goes to the hospital? How? How did she pick us? I didn't even know we were being considered."

"Yes, you can be at the hospital and she picked you because why wouldn't she? Now call Stephen!"

It's close to nine when Jen and Avery pull up to their mailbox. "Brush your teeth and get your jammies on right away," Jen says, pulling the mail from the box.

"No stories?"

Jen pulls into the garage. "One. Rehearsal went too late to read lots of them tonight."

They walk into the back hallway, where Avery kicks off her tennis shoes into the coat closet, before going to the bathroom. Jen sets her purse and mail on the kitchen counter as she takes off her coat, hanging it on the back of a chair at the table. She grabs the stack of mail and begins to sort it, throwing several pieces into the trash. An envelope with Avery's name on the front stops her and she feels her breath catch, reading the return address: "Heaven." She flips the envelope over and looks for a return address there. "What in the . . . ?" Avery has put on her pajamas, the nightie with colorful hearts on it, and is sitting on the sofa, holding a book. Jen carries the letter into the living room and sits next to her. "This is for you," she says, handing her the letter.

Avery rips open the envelope and pulls out the most beautiful stationery she's ever seen. It's almost transparent with iridescent flecks of silver and gold. It feels like silk in her hands. "Wow!" she says, touching the edges with a golden thread running around the border. She looks at her mom. The writing is a calligraphy of sorts, too fancy for her to sound out. "Can you read it?"

" 'Dear Avery,' " Jen reads. " 'I wanted you to know right away that I received your letter on its way to Heaven.' " Avery gasps and Jen's heart fills to her throat.

Your mom is right, your dad is very happy. Few people know that Heaven is greater than Neverland or anything you've seen in the movies. It is the most remarkable, cool, amazing place ever. God isn't grumpy or mean but awesome to be with and every day is even better than Christmas. She's also right when she told you that your dad would have stayed longer if he could but his leaving had nothing to do with you. It wasn't your fault. Your dad is very proud of you; he has always been very proud of you and wants you to live a full life of joy, happiness, peace, and walking with God. I am so glad that I got to be the angel to answer your letter. You see, although others have floated past me, I was never able to catch one. I am so happy that I caught yours. I will carry it in my heart forever. Thank you for trusting me with it.

Merry Christmas,
One of God's angels

Avery holds the letter, staring at it and then smiles. "I never thought I'd get a letter from an angel." She looks at Jen. "Did you?"

Jen wipes at the stream of tears at the side of her nose with the back of her hand and laughs. "No, I sure didn't."

"It's awesome, isn't it?" Her eyes are wide and her face is glowing.

"It is so awesome!"

They snuggle together on the sofa in the light of the Christmas tree and trace their fingers over the words, reading the letter again. Avery is filled with questions: *Where in the universe did the angel catch her letter? How old is the angel? Is it a boy or girl or a fierce, warring angel that had just fought an enormous battle and had taken a break when it caught the letter?* Avery wonders if its clothes are golden or shimmery silver like the angel choir's and what exactly the wings look like.

Jen knows there are no wings or flowing golden robes on this angel but rather a pair of jeans or khaki pants or a simple skirt and sweater that is attached to a mortgage and a used car and a life of ups and downs, victories and near misses. She'll never know this angel's name or where he or she lives or works or goes to school. She'll never know where the letter was found or how the "angel" tracked them down but some things are not meant to be known, only to be believed.

FIFTEEN

These people who live in darkness will see a great light. They live in a place covered with the shadows of death, but a light will shine on them.

— MATTHEW 4:16

The shrubs in front of the church are sparkling with white lights and the walkway to the steps is glowing with bagged candles. The lobby is also aglow with candles, lighted wreaths, and a stunning tree. Although he goes to church across town, Ray Elhart picks one of his biggest and best trees each year to donate to Bill, his longtime high school friend and pastor of Grandon Community Church. Ray and his wife, Rita, stand near it, observing fallen needles and calculating how many days the tree has left. When you own a Christmas tree farm, you never look at a Christmas tree the same way again.

A group of men, including Gloria's husband, Marshall, and women and children are busy handing out cups of warm, spiced cider and battery-operated candles for the final song. Gloria and Miriam watch as the crowd filters into the sanctuary for the first service of the Nativity. Miriam is stunning in a red angora sweater, simple pearls, and black slacks. Gloria is beaming in her best Christmas sweater, a green cotton blend knit that Miriam bought for her last year with the word "hope" written in Christmas ornaments across the front.

"Ready?" Gloria asks.

Miriam sticks her head through a sanctuary door, watching people file into their seats. "My body is covered with a sort of mist."

Gloria looks at her, dumbfounded. "You mean you're sweating?"

"Don't be crass, Gloria! I'm misting."

Jennifer, Lily, and Ryan stand in the lobby and greet people as they stamp snow off their shoes at the front door and await their cue from Miriam to bring in the angel choir.

Lily smiles as Kaylee and her parents walk through the door, brushing snow from their scarves and coats. "You came," Lily says, hugging her. "Hi, I'm Lily," she says to Kaylee's parents. Her mom smiles and it's

Kaylee's mouth. Her eyes are from her dad.

"She's told us about you," her mom says, gripping Lily's hand. "I'm Joni. This is my husband, Ben."

"Here," Lily says, reaching for three candles. "These are for 'Silent Night,' the final song." She looks at Kaylee. "Maybe I'll see you after."

"Is Stephen here?" Kaylee asks.

Lily nods. "He's helping in the back, keeping the smallest members of the angel choir entertained." She looks at Joni and Ben. "It takes a village." She walks them to the doors of the sanctuary. "Sit anywhere you're comfortable."

A man with a guitar takes his place at the front and begins to play "What Child Is This?" as the crowd filters in. The look of terror in Miriam's eyes tells Lily, Jen, and Ryan that it's time to line up the choir, as she takes the actors to their places. The thirty-member choir looks lovely in their silvery, white, and gold robes. They are careful to keep their candles upright. Avery, Sofia, and the other children are shiny and vibrant and their faces radiant, even the Ramsey triplets with their messy hair and dirty tennis shoes. "Sing out! Sing out!" Miriam mouths from across the lobby. The triplets mimic her and she claps her hands together one final time to get their attention. She raises an eyebrow and then smiles, standing up straight as she wants them to do. She races toward the shepherds, where a camouflage shirt can be seen beneath one of their robes. Miriam tucks and pins and makes a noise like a growl.

"We climbed out of the tree stands early so we could get here on time," one of them says, in a sheepish whisper.

She looks him and the others over, a ragamuffin group of hunters with hairy faces and rough hands, who undoubtedly would have been called upon by angels on that night so long ago, and smiles, giving him a solid pat on the shoulder. Pastor Bill can be heard welcoming everyone to Grandon Community and blessing them with the peace of Christmas. The musicians begin the music for "Sing Noel" and the choir hits the first note, clean and sharp, just as they have practiced, and they file into the sanctuary, lining the walls and the aisles, the candles lighting their faces in the darkened church. One of the triplets, Miriam has no idea if it is number one, two, or three, catches a glimpse of the choir's shadows on the walls and holds his fingers up behind his candle to make shadow puppets. The other triplets join in as the adult choir members nearby try to stop them. Miriam waves at them from the back of the church and groans when several audience members begin to giggle.

The choir remains in place for "O Holy Night" and Kaylee gazes at the faces around her, listening. They don't look like a religious crowd, whatever that means, but there is a sense that, even amid the giggling and the shadow puppets, that this is somehow a holy time and a holy place. It's a feeling she can't describe but it sits there, stirring just under her chest. She looks at the faces of the angel choir, the lean, the dark skinned, the round middles, the high-bridged noses holding glasses, and the bright eyes of children. One child with pale skin and a mass of red curls catches her attention, standing in the aisle next to her row. The girl seems to peer into Kaylee's eyes and the eyes around her, as if she's looking for someone. Her face is bright, huge and full, earnest with searching. Was it this face? Or perhaps that one? For whatever reason, her little face grips Kaylee because in that fleeting moment, she realizes the child isn't looking for someone after all but actually sees the face she's looking for. The face is here in her seat and right next to her in her mom and dad's seats, standing in the doorway, looking for an empty spot, or walking the streets in a drunken stupor. The child seems to see the face that Kaylee is searching for, the one the pastor just moments before called Immanuel, God with us. The face she's looking for was there at the beginning and is here now, looking for her and the others around her, calling each name and extending His hand through the sounds of this angel choir. The little girl moves on, her voice touching Kaylee's arm and her mother's hair.

Mary and Joseph say each of their lines in such a way that Miriam feels her face beaming, but as she watches the scene unfold, she notices strands of long orange hair fall onto Audrey's shoulder. When Audrey reaches for the baby, her costume moves ever so slightly and reveals the tiger's head on Audrey's neck.

"The tiger's out," she whispers, hissing at Gloria. "The mother of Jesus looks like a carnival act from Bethlehem!" Gloria covers her mouth and Miriam's eyes flame. "This is not funny, Gloria! It's tragic!"

"No one is looking at her tattoo," Gloria says. "They're listening to her."

Miriam stands on her tiptoes to see the audience's reaction. They are listening. Even the triplets, who are swaying back and forth to some unheard Christmas song inside their heads, are listening.

For a moment or an hour or two, the gloom of cynicism and doubt are pushed back a little, as the scenes of Mary and Joseph, the shepherds struck by wonder, and the angels who lit up the sky with blazing light, play out as either myth or something worth believing. Kaylee catches Lily's eye, standing with Stephen, back in the doorway. They believe with all their hearts; she can tell.

"Listen to me!" the Angel of the Lord shouts. "*The* baby of all babies has been born!" Miriam flinches at the sheer volume of his voice but the audience applauds. Triplet One takes a bow and then waves his finger in the air as if this proclamation is one that should go on and on.

As the notes of "Hark! The Herald Angels Sing" soar to the ceiling, Kaylee wonders how even an unbeliever can't believe in something, especially at this time of year. There *is* peace on earth, somewhere. There *is* goodwill toward men in many places throughout the earth. There *are* dreams and hopes. The wonder of being a child *does* exist, along with new beginnings and the great light of Christmas. Here, among these people, she feels it. Her throat tightens and she stifles a cry. She reaches for her belly and gasps.

"Are you okay?" her mother whispers.

"Yeah, just a weird pain." Her face registers shock and is twisted in a grimace.

Her mom looks at her dad and says, "Grab our coats. We need to go."

"No," Kaylee whispers. "I'm fine. I want to hear the last few songs." The choir begins to sing "Jesus, Oh What a Wonderful Child" and Kaylee relaxes, the pain subsiding.

The shepherds and angels have gathered around the stable and Mary smiles. Miriam realizes, watching Mary struggle as she holds the baby, that she never had Audrey practice holding a live baby. It was always a doll. The baby reaches for Audrey's costume and pulls it down off her head, revealing the entire tiger's head. Audrey is too busy trying to keep the baby still to worry about her costume. Miriam touches her face and realizes that sweat is dripping down her temples. She is appalled and flinches as she dabs at the sweat with the sleeve of her angora sweater.

As the choir begins "Go Tell It on the Mountain," Bunker makes his way to the center of the stage. Miriam holds her breath as he opens his mouth. The sound is that of a dog whining for supper but Bunker catches the tune before it turns into a long, bellowing howl and sways to the music. The audience applauds his effort and he pumps a fist into the air. As the last notes fade, Kaylee reaches for her stomach again.

"Okay, that's it," her mom says. "We need to go."

"Mom, I really want to hear this."

"We can move to the lobby and you can listen there." Her mom's eyes are sincere and urgent and Kaylee stands, making her way out of the row with her parents.

"I'm fine," Kaylee says, as her dad opens the door for the lobby. "I just felt weird in there for a —" She grabs her belly again and reaches for her dad's arm. "What's happening?"

"Ben! Get the car!"

"I really want to hear the end," Kaylee says, her breath coming in short gasps.

"Sweetie, you are in labor. We have to go."

Kaylee looks around, her eyes scanning the lobby. "I want to find Lily. She was standing at the door on the other side. Mom, please!"

Joni rushes to the other side of the lobby in an effort to find Lily. "Is Lily here?" she asks, in the direction of Jennifer and Ryan, hoping someone will volunteer to help.

"She was just here," Jennifer says.

"My daughter is in labor and wants to see her."

Jennifer races inside the sanctuary and Ryan keeps step with Joni, as she runs to Kaylee. "That's our car," Joni says to Ryan, looking outside.

Ryan takes hold of Kaylee's arm as Joni takes the other and they usher her toward the exit. Ryan is helping her into the car when Jennifer, Lily, and Stephen bound through the doors. "Please get her to the hospital on time," Ryan says, starting to close the car door, but when Kaylee sees Lily, she reaches out to stop him.

"That was beautiful. In there," Kaylee says.

Lily smiles. "It was, wasn't it?" Kaylee's face scrunches in pain and Lily grabs her arm. "Go! Go!"

"Please come," Kaylee says, between breaths. "Both of you. You have to be there!"

Lily looks at Stephen and his eyes are huge and surprised. "Of course we'll come. We'll be there as soon as we can," Lily says.

Kaylee shakes her head. "You have to come now. You have to come inside the delivery room."

Lily looks at Stephen, Ryan, and Jennifer. "That's very sweet but your parents —"

Kaylee grabs her hand. "You need to be

there for the birth of your baby."

"What? I —"

"You'll be there, right?"

"Yes! Yes!" Lily shouts, closing the door.

Lily and Stephen and Jen and Ryan watch as the car pulls away. Inside the church, the message of the birth of *the* child into the darkness of the world is ending, as a new light is about to shine. They don't fold their arms against the cold or brush the snow from their sweaters or wipe it from their hair but rather begin to laugh in the chill.

Lily and Stephen are directed to the fourth floor and race past the nurses' station, draped with tinsel and ornaments, and through the halls where they see Kaylee and her parents. "The doctor said I need to try to walk," Kaylee says. "I don't know why. I never liked taking walks before so why would I like it when I'm this pregnant?"

Lily laughs and wraps her arms around Kaylee. Her eyes are full and she smiles, shaking her head. "I don't even know where to —"

"Please, let's go inside," Ben says, motioning to a room. He helps Kaylee to the bed and Joni props the pillows behind her back.

"That day I saw you at the bakery, you were meeting with a woman from the adoption agency," Kaylee says.

"Dorothy," Stephen says.

"I didn't know her but Mom and I were headed to the adoption agency after lunch that day. We walked right into Dorothy's office and I knew immediately why you were meeting with her and I knew that I wanted you to have my baby."

Tears fall faster than Lily can keep up with and she grabs Kaylee's hand, sitting next to her on the bed. "When I met you I assumed you were keeping the baby."

"I thought that for a while, but every time I thought it I also thought, 'You're sixteen. What do you know about raising a kid?' " She looks at her mom and Joni's eyes are wet. "And my parents are still raising theirs. I knew that somebody was out there who would love the baby. I just didn't know who. But then I met you." Lily laughs through her tears and wipes at them with her finger. Ben reaches for the tissues and hands her the box. "On that very first night I met you, you said that I had followed a nudge to the church. I think I did, too."

Lily blows her nose and looks up at Ben and Joni and then at Kaylee. "I thought you were due in February."

"That's what the doctor thought but I never could give a date of when I got pregnant. In the last three weeks, he said the baby would definitely be here sooner and that's when I knew I had to get to the adoption agency." She smiles, looking at Stephen. "I hope you're ready to be parents."

He steps next to the bed. "We've been ready. We've been waiting a long time." He looks at Kaylee and works at keeping his face on straight. "Thank you."

Ben and Joni struggle to smile. This is their first grandchild and they know they won't be a part of its life, not in the way they'd always imagined, and that's a hurt they'll have to learn to live with — a part of their hearts will be missing. They look at one another and at Kaylee and a tear sneaks out of Joni's eye. Kaylee will remember this day and think of this child so many times throughout her life. How could such an exciting time feel so sad?

Kaylee has that feeling beneath her chest again, the one she had as the Angel of the Lord said, "Listen to me! *The* baby of all babies has been born!" and she holds her mother's hand, letting tears fill her eyes.

Sixteen

Grief never ends . . . But it changes. It's a passage, not a place to stay. Grief is not a sign of weakness, nor a lack of faith. It is the price of love.

— AUTHOR UNKNOWN

Gloria and Marshall's house is filled with angel choir members, along with "Joseph" and his real wife, Lucie, and "Mary" and her boyfriend, Liam. Members of the hunting club stand by the fire discussing four-wheelers, land leases, and compound bows while the Ramsey triplets shake presents beneath the tree. "Andrew, if you unwrap other people's presents," Miriam says, passing through to the kitchen, "you end up on Santa's naughty list for life." The triplets unhand the gifts and follow her to the cookies.

"You got one of our names right," Andrew says, looking up at her.

"And it only took three weeks and one million gray hairs." She watches as they dismantle the cookie arrangement and sighs. "I'd love to say that I'm going to miss them," she says to Gloria. "But if I did, that would make me —"

"A liar," Gloria says.

"Well, I was going to say 'sentimental' but 'liar' works, too."

Gloria laughs, pouring herself and Miriam a cup of spiced cider. "To a wonderful Nativity," she says, handing a cup to Miriam. "It was touching and beautiful and brought Christmas to life."

"Gloria, it was, in your words, a hot mess! Whatever will the church do to us?"

"Ask us to head it up again next year!" Gloria says.

They both cackle with laughter and Miriam looks into her cup, groaning. "Is this the strongest drink that you have? At the very least, don't you have any eggnog?"

"There are children," Gloria says, opening her arms.

She rolls her eyes. "Oh! I'm so sick of children."

Gloria throws her head back, laughing.

When Avery arrives, Sofia grabs her hand and runs to the kitchen. They slip two pieces of chocolate chess pie onto plates before scurrying to a corner of the kitchen, where they sit together on the floor. "I am feeling just like the innkeeper," Gloria says, watching them. "There's plenty," she says to Jen. "Fill up a plate and find a seat or a place on the floor!"

Louis Armstrong's " 'Zat You, Santa Claus" fills the home and the house smells like burning wood, cider, coffee, cookies, and ham. "Any word from Lily yet?" Jen asks, reaching for a plate.

Gloria reaches for her phone in the back pocket of her jeans. "Nothing yet but I've got my phone on vibrate in case I don't hear it."

Miriam raises her brows. "And you're suggesting you can feel it through all that padding?"

Gloria looks at Jen. "Not even Christmas makes her nice."

Jen takes her plate of food and searches the living room, before heading to the den. The room is dark but he's here, looking out the window. "Hi," Jen says. Ryan turns, smiling. "Is it snowing?"

"No. There's a star or a planet. It's huge."

She steps next to him and looks up. "Our very own Bethlehem star." She looks into her cup. "That's what Avery called it when we were driving over here."

"She's a pretty awesome little girl."

"She is." She looks into the sky with him. "She's so much like Michael!" He nods, holding his cup. "He died three and a half years ago."

He turns to look at her. "Your husband . . ."

"In June. When we'd gotten up that morning, I reminded him of the hallway bathroom toilet. It had been running for several days and he kept telling me he'd fix it. That morning, he said he'd pick up a pizza for all of us after work. It was Friday and our pizza night. Avery loved it. She still does. He said he'd fix the toilet after we ate our pizza. He collapsed at work, and a few hours later, he died in the hospital. A faulty heart that he didn't know about. I never heard the toilet running after that. The noise was still there but I didn't hear it anymore."

Ryan leans against the window, facing her. "I thought your husband . . . I mean, Avery talked about him like . . ."

She smiles. "Avery's had a rough time. Michael's death really didn't sink in until a year or so ago. For some reason, everything just caught up with her and she couldn't wrap her head around it. She was so confused. So sad."

"Is she going to be okay?"

Light from the moon and the stars fall on her face. "Yes. She's heard from her very own angel." He is confused and she smiles. "It's a long story but somewhere out there, there's an angel who's probably sitting by a fire drinking eggnog with a house full of family and friends, with no idea of what a simple letter meant to a little girl at Christmas. She never got to say good-bye to Michael. The last she heard from him was that we were going to have pizza and he was going to play Candyland with her. Now she has some sort of closure."

He turns, leaning against the window. "That day when we were working on the set and I said that I thought it would be easier if Julie were no longer here . . . I didn't mean that. I would never mean that."

"I know."

"I don't know how that would devastate Sofia." He watches her. "Or how it has devastated Avery. I can't imagine the last three and a half years for either of you."

She shakes her head. "It's been worse than I could have imagined — the loneliness I feel without him. You know, picking up the phone to tell him something or turning to see his reaction after Avery does something funny but he isn't here. We always talked in bed before Avery got up but there's no one to talk to anymore. His voice, his laugh, his hugs are no longer here. Part of my heart and my body are missing and I can't get it back."

"I'm sorry he's gone."

She nods. "But in a lot of ways it's been better than I could have imagined. So many people helped us at just the right time. Things like mowing our yard and painting the outside of our house or Marshall showing me how Michael did all of our bills online. In the weeks following Michael's death, during that time when people would still drop by or call, someone fixed the toilet. I don't even know who did it. But one day I woke up and realized it was quiet, and in a strange way I missed the sound because it was the last thing that Michael was going to do." She shakes her head. "Time doesn't heal all wounds. I don't know who first said that, but they were wrong. It can't heal all wounds but people sure help ease the pain."

He's looking out the window, thinking. "What was Michael like?"

"He was funny. He liked to tease me and Avery. He could really get her giggling — much better than I can. He loved sports, especially football. He always watched it but actually played basketball." She smiles, remembering. "He played on a rec league and was a crazy man out on the court. He liked to fly-fish with his dad, he loved food, especially good pizza, and he liked to mow the lawn. He actually looked forward to it in the summer." She looks into her cup. "He was a good man although not without faults; he had plenty of them that he spoke plainly about but he was a great man who left this world too soon." Her eyes are wet and she and Ryan stand in the quiet. They hear Avery and Sofia laughing in the living room and smile, listening to them. "Avery's going to miss seeing Sofia."

"Even if she sees her every day at school?"

Jen glances up at him. "I thought you settled on the job with the company in Riverside."

He shakes his head. "We couldn't come to an agreement on benefits and Sofia really loves it here. We found a house two blocks from here on the same day that Hazelton offered me more money. It just made sense."

She smiles, listening to Avery's and Sofia's voices rise and fall. "Would you and Sofia be open to having Christmas dinner with Avery and me tomorrow?"

He nods. "That'd be great."

Jen is about to say more when one of the triplets yells from the living room, "Another baby is here!" She and Ryan move to the doorway and see Gloria and the triplets, standing in the middle of the room, looking at her phone. "Robert Layton has just texted me about Lily. He's her father, you know?"

"Everyone knows," Miriam hisses, waving her hand in the air for her to get on with it. "What did she have?"

"Jonathan Robert is the newest citizen of Grandon!" Cheers erupt from the party and Gloria lifts her cup. "To Lily and Stephen's new life and to the wonderful young woman who gave it to them and a very merry Christmas to all!"

Ryan and Jen and everyone in the living room lift their cups and shout, *"Merry Christmas!"*

Seventeen

All the darkness in the world cannot extinguish the light of a single candle.

— Saint Francis of Assisi

Jen and Avery sit on the living room floor, playing with Avery's new tea set, as Perry Como sings in the background. Avery slept in Jen's room last night, where they watched *A Charlie Brown Christmas* before talking about Michael's Christmas in heaven.

"What will he eat?" Avery had asked.

"The best food ever!" Jen said, pulling the blankets up to Avery's neck and lying on her side so they could talk.

"Chocolate pie?"

Jen smiled. "With no calories! Peanut butter fudge, sugar cookies with icing and sprinkles, and stuff we've never even heard of before."

"Like what?" Her eyes were sleepy.

"I don't know, because we've never heard

of it but, boy, is it awesome! So yummy!"

"With marshmallows and chocolate?"

Jen nodded, her eyes were bright. "Biggest, fluffiest, tastiest marshmallows ever!"

"I want some."

Jen laughed. "Me, too! But we'll have to wait and just let Dad have them for now."

Avery turned her face upward and shouted, "Merry Christmas, Dad!" Jen smiled and Avery looked at her. "Sad or happy tears, Mom?"

"Happy," she said, kissing Avery's face.

The light has returned to Avery's eyes, and although Jen knows there will be troubled days ahead, filled with homework woes, jealousies, hurt feelings, mean girls, and boyfriend angst, she is grateful. There is enough light to walk out with.

She smells the ham and jumps up to look inside the crockpot. "Hope this tastes as good as it looks. First time for everything," she says, closing the lid. "Would you like to mash the potatoes when it's time?"

Avery's head pops up next to the coffee table. "Do I have to?"

"No," Jen says, laughing. "I'm kidding." She spots the angel's letter to Avery on the countertop and picks it up, reading over the words again before propping it against the wall, behind a picture of her, Avery, and

Michael.

"When are we eating, Mom? I'm getting hungry!"

"Very soon! You'll have enough time to get out of your jammies and put on some nice clothes."

"Nice clothes?"

The doorbell rings and Jen laughs, walking toward the door. "No! Like I could ever get you out of jammies today!"

Avery bolts for the door, opening it with a flourish. She reaches for Sofia's arms, which are full of her own toys, and pulls her inside. "Look what I got!"

"Are we too early?" Ryan asks, holding two wrapped gifts.

"No. Come in," Jen says.

He follows her inside and they watch the girls, reveling in their new toys. He holds the presents out. "For you and Avery."

She takes them and sets them on the coffee table. "Thank you."

Her eyes look blue today and her hair hasn't been brushed but rather pulled back into a quick ponytail. She is close and he breathes in her perfume. She is lovely and perfect.

"Would you like something to drink?" she asks, leading him to the kitchen.

"Not yet. I had about four cups of coffee

and eggnog at Aunt Gloria's for breakfast." He sits at the table and his eyes land on the rainbow-colored, woolen scarf around her neck, straining to see something on the end of it.

She catches him staring. "What's wrong?"

He shakes his head. "Nothing. It looked like there was something on the end of your scarf."

She takes the chair across from him and holds the end of the scarf out "This?" He looks at the monogram: RM.

"That looks like . . . Where?" He can't find the words.

"Three years ago, Avery and I were in a car accident." He sits back in the chair, listening. "We were twenty miles from Grandon and it was pitch-black out on the highway. A stranger prayed for us that night and gave me this scarf and Avery an angel doll. That was you."

He rubs his face with both palms, reaching for words. "Wow . . . I . . . I don't . . . That was you? How did you know it was me?"

"It came together in pieces. First, I remembered your look when you saw the angel doll that Avery gave Sofia." She picks up the end of the scarf. "I thought this belonged to a man with the fire and rescue department, who was first on the scene of the accident. His name even matched these initials. But he was adamant it wasn't him. Then, I remembered seeing this exact scarf on Sofia when you walked through the door at Gloria's, the night I was there doing the sewing. I didn't think anything about it then. I just couldn't imagine how the 'RM' on this scarf could be you, but last night when you were closing the car door, it sounded like you said, 'Please get her to the hospital on time.' I realized later that you weren't talking to her dad — because of course he'd do everything possible to get her there on time — but that it was a quick prayer. It was so quick I could have missed it. It all came together then. After the Nativity, I was helping Avery with her coat and the scarf and I held on to it to make sure the initials really said 'RM.' "

He sits back in the chair, looking at her and then at the girls in the living room. "I don't even know what to . . ." He shakes his head and exhales. "I had remodeled Gloria and Marshall's upstairs bathroom and was leaving Grandon that night, heading home, when I stopped and got Sofia that angel doll on Main Street. I knew she'd be asleep when I got home, but I was going to give it to her when she woke up the next day. That was the night that Julie left. I never thought another thing about the doll. All these years and I never remembered giving it away. And I never thought another thing about the scarf. Julie's parents gave it to me and I never liked it. They gave a matching scarf to Julie. Sofia loves to wear it." He looks at her and shakes his head again. "This is . . . I don't know how to wrap my mind around it."

"Maybe we're not supposed to." She takes a breath, looking at him. "For the last couple of years I've been searching for answers about Michael's death. What signs did we miss about his heart? Did he ignore any symptoms that I didn't know about? Our therapist told me I'll probably never have those answers. For the longest time, I even blamed the doctors who tried to save Michael's life. I'd walk through my days so angry at them, even though I knew deep inside that they did everything they could. I wondered how many of them went home that day and suffered because they couldn't save Michael? In the last few weeks I've thanked everyone who helped Michael that day. I know they did everything they could. And when I started doing that I realized that I wanted to thank everyone who helped Avery and me at the accident scene. I've been looking for you for weeks. And here you are." He shakes his head, smiling. "Thank you. For your simple kindness to us that night."

He tilts his head and says, "What's strange is that on the way home that night I thought, 'I'm so grateful that I wasn't in that accident.' And then when Julie told me that she'd met another man, I felt as if I'd been struck harder than any of you in those cars. Days afterward, I actually thought that you had it so much easier because you were getting out of that accident alive and I felt like a dead man. I remember how creepy the highway felt because it was so dark and the moon was hidden behind clouds, making it hard to see, but my life actually felt darker when she said she was leaving. For months, I walked around with this" — he moves his hands in the air — "awful anger hanging over me. There was this great storm of hate and bitterness that threatened to break me and I think it would have if it hadn't been for Sofia. Sometimes she'd take hold of my hand as we were walking through a hardware store or somewhere else and I felt as if I could float away if I let go of her hand, so I'd hold on tighter." He looks over at her playing with Avery in the living room. "She kept me sane."

Jen nods. "I know. Avery kept me sane. She's helped me in so many ways to get up and to keep going every day. Even on her hardest days, she helped me go on."

"Sofia kept me from saying vicious things about Julie or Derek." He looks at Jen. "Julie's husband. She helped me realize that our lives are going to overlap, no matter how much I didn't want them to." He looks at her. "But lives overlap and mingle in ways I'm only beginning to understand."

She smiles, nodding. "Is Gabrielle —"

He doesn't let her finish. "No. Whatever it is you were going to ask. No."

"I'm glad you took the job with Hazelton and found a house here."

"Me, too."

The girls beg them to come into the living room and Jen and Ryan sit on the sofa, where the gifts that Ryan brought still sit on the coffee table. They watch their girls and listen to them laugh, as the dinner rolls rise and Charles Brown begs his baby to "Please Come Home for Christmas." She reaches over and wraps her hand around his three middle fingers. They sit this way, letting the music and laughter fill the room. They will get to eating, just as they will get to tomorrow and to moving furniture into Ryan and Sofia's new home, and to starting over and enrolling in school, and to opening the gifts on the table. They will get to all of it.

In time.

ABOUT THE AUTHOR

Donna VanLiere is *The New York Times* and *USA Today* bestselling author of *The Good Dream, Finding Grace, The Angels of Morgan Hill* and eight Christmas books, including the perennial favorites *The Christmas Shoes* and *The Christmas Hope*. She travels as a speaker and lives in Franklin, Tennessee, with her husband and three children.